Editing: Elemental Editing & Proofreading

Internal Art: Jeanne Bradley

Cover Art: Fantastical Ink

❀ Created with Vellum

WAR CROWN

ELIZABETH BROWN

Pronunciation Guide

ASHERA: A·SHEER·A

MALACHI: MA·LUH·KAI

JACOBI: JA·CO·BI

DUNYA: DOON·YAH

SHAYTAN: SHAY·TAN

MASAS: MAH·SAS

MALAK: MAL·LAC

JUNIYA: JU·NEE·YAH

QAMAR: KAH·MAR

SAHIRA: SA·HERE·A

N
W   E
S

SHAYTAN

QAMAR

MALAK

JUNIYA

MASAS

SAHIRA

DUNYA

ACKNOWLEDGMENTS

To Sin and Scar... Thank you both so fucking much! I would not have been able to finish this damn book without you!

As always, to my husband and son (and now to the TWO new ones on the way). You guys keep me going. I love you!

To Julia—Bish... I love the shit out of you.

TRIGGER WARNINGS

The author is not responsible for any children begot from reading this book. She is also not responsible for any overused toys, dead batteries, or over heating.

WARNING THIS BOOK CONTAINS THE FOLLOWING:

- Explicit sex
- Blood play
- Knife play
- Explicit death scenes
- Emotional distress

1

AMBROSE

The clearest indication of a small cock—and someone's need to overcompensate for it—was the illusion of control in the form of public humiliation. I'd never participated in a public spectacle because, unlike my father, I had nothing to compensate for.

I was the only heir my father had been able to produce, despite a large harem of concubines, and I'd always had the feeling that this was intentional. I was sure his logic went something like this: If he only had one heir, that son was less likely to conspire with anyone to kill him. They'd forever be grateful for being the crowned prince and living the life of absolute luxury he had provided.

What a load of shit.

My life had been anything but luxurious. Growing up in my father's court, I'd been subjected to endless assassination attempts by men I knew worked for my father. My mother taught me early on to keep my ambitions, especially for the crown, close to my vest. If I planned to make any sort of power move, I shouldn't make it until I was completely certain I'd succeed. She knew the best way for me to survive to adulthood was to keep my head down until I came into my power. Only then, she'd said, should I make a statement loud enough to ensure that my father never tried to fuck with me again.

I could only listen to her so much. She'd grown too ambitious herself, which had earned her the honor of her carcass being tossed onto the streets where she'd *been picked apart by dogs. I'd been forced to walk by it day after day. My father had wanted that lesson to stick, and it had.*

I'd waited. I'd watched. I'd listened. I'd trained. I'd learned.

Everything I'd done had been for this moment—my first feeding.

Like most supernaturals, vampires didn't fully come into our powers until we hit puberty. It had something to do with stress on our bodies or some such nonsense. Whatever the reason, I'd had to pretend I was a weakling for almost twenty years. I planned on making my first feeding fucking memorable.

Thankfully my father and his need to overcompensate provided a solid assist in that area. He'd decided that my first feeding should be in front of the entire court. He'd even allowed commoners to attend. The prick.

I stood in front of my father, who was seated in his large, black throne on the raised center of the room—again, clearly overcompensating. It was unfortunate that we looked nearly identical with the same dark curly hair, same ruby red eyes, and same pale skin. The copper lanterns that hung from the ceiling were dimmed for dramatic effect and tilted in such a way that my father was brightly illuminated. Tomas's need to always be the center of attention never surprised anyone, and he always filled his court with sycophants. His desire was so great, the light was always angled away from the ornate tapestries that hung around the room. They told the story of my father's rise to power, of how he—as one of the original beings—was created by the gods. That was an even bigger load of shit. Yes, my father was old, but he had no real knowledge of the gods, and no real knowledge of Dunya beyond Masas' borders. Wouldn't an original being have unparalleled knowledge of such matters? Then again, my father needed to assert his imaginary power over the people through weak public displays committed by others, so it made sense that he would attempt to gain legitimacy through the gods.

On a dais next to the throne sat my family's ceremonial sword. Despite my father's claims, I highly doubted he'd ever actually used that monstrosity in battle. It was far too large to wield properly. The jewels on the hilt made it far too uncomfortable to hold for long periods of time. If anything, it was yet another way for my father to compensate. Pathetic.

My father gestured to the courtyard displayed through the large, floor to ceiling window on the other side of the room. Dutifully, all heads turned in that direction.

"Behold! I present my heir with five thousand blood slaves for his first feed-

ing!" Quiet murmurs went up around the room. No vampire had ever made it through so many on their first feeding. I was sure most assumed it wasn't possible. "He may take as many as he pleases!"

I didn't bother to stop the smirk that spread across my face. I inhaled deeply as I turned back to face the vampire king lounging on his throne. He had a smug expression stamped across his features. The prick wanted me to fail. Challenge accepted.

Without a word, I spun on my heel and made my way into the courtyard. I'd take them all.

And take them all I did. Despite not wanting to be part of a public spectacle, I knew that I needed to send a message to the old man, a very fucking clear message—I was more powerful than him, so he should watch his fucking back.

In front of the entire court, for an entire week without rest, I fed, fucked, beat, tortured, and killed all five thousand blood slaves. I drained each one dry just to make Tomas sweat.

When I returned to the throne room, drenched in blood, and stood once again before my father, I knew I'd clearly displayed my strength. The court was buzzing, and all eyes were glued to me as I folded my arms across my chest. He'd wanted me to appear weak before the court. Now, the old fools knew that I was unquestionably the legitimate heir to Masas' throne.

I could see the cogs in my father's head turning as he attempted to spin my prowess to reflect on him and not me. Let him. I had every intention of allowing him to dig his own grave. I planned to take everything he'd built and torch his legacy.

"My son!" Tomas's overly excited exclamation exaggerated the false undertones in his voice. He held his arms out as if to embrace me, but I leaned back. "He has demonstrated his strength and ability to rule all of Masas one day!"

The roar of the crowd rang through the room, nearly deafening with the people's excitement. I wanted to roll my eyes but kept my features stony and detached. My father's gaze was fixed on me, studying me for any reaction I might let slip, anything he could potentially use against me. I'd been far too careful to let anything show now.

"You honor me, Father. I can only hope to be as powerful as you one day." I smiled as I took his hands in mine.

I felt him tense. That was right asshole, I was coming for you. After that little display, I knew I wouldn't need any of his bullshit to maintain power over my people. No. My people would come to fear my displeasure. They would come to understand that I was their god and that they had no need for the gods of old.

Tomas presented me with an obsidian blade. This was a typical gift for one who had finished their first feeding, particularly amongst the nobility. It was meant to symbolize everything we were as vampires—stunningly dark with lethal beauty. The blade would never dull and, if made correctly, spells would have no effect on it. I was sure he thought his gift honored me, but it disgusted me. I would keep it close in the hopes that one day I would slit his throat with it, then I'd burn it with everything else his reign had touched.

～

It took two centuries for my plans to come to fruition. For over two hundred years, I plotted and schemed before I finally began to wrestle power from my father. I'd started slowly, befriending the palace staff before painstakingly working my way through the ranks. By the time I made it to the nobility, my father had become too sick to truly rule. I owned the people's fear, so it was time to show them who their god was. To hell with gaining their love or respect.

I would rule through my fury and the people's terror, through blood and sex. My court would show Dunya what it truly meant to be a vampire, and we'd let nothing stand in our way. Our streets would run red with blood. I could already taste it.

I'd had all that. Until I met her.

Ashera.

She was a queen who hadn't needed to hide in the shadows and manipulate or scheme. She'd openly stood against her king, paid for her crown in blood, and had somehow earned more loyalty through her rebellion than I ever had through my reign of terror.

Ashera had shown me a different way to rule. A better way. And now who was attempting to take the throne from her? None other than Tomas, the slimy bastard who had played me like the overconfident, cocky fool I was. I'd thought him too sick, too weak to rule, and he'd let me believe that.

It was only after Ashera had ascended to the throne in Shaytan that he'd shown even the smallest spark of life. It seemed like the thought of a woman on the throne, especially one who demanded freedom for mortals, was something worth getting out of bed for. According to Tomas, Ashera had two strikes against her. She was missing the most important possession a ruler could have—a cock— and I, the son who simultaneously disgusted and terrified him, was her mate.

I couldn't help but wonder if my old and horribly ill father had been merely biding his time while I played at ruling Masas. Had he planned to retake control, setting me up for failure? Or had he truly been so frail that only the thought of a female *on the throne was enough to magically heal him just to see her and her supporters ripped to pieces?*

I didn't know, and I didn't care. I was going to tear him apart, limb from limb, before slitting his throat with that fucking obsidian blade and watching him drown in a pool of his own blood. If he was lucky, I'd let him watch me fuck my little queen in his blood before I carved out his eyes.

Then again, maybe not.

~

MY EYES SNAPPED OPEN, my chest rapidly rising and falling as I blinked to get my bearings. I was in bed, the cramped one we all shared with Ashera in Thorne's home in Qamar. I stared at the ceiling, my mind racing as memories assaulted me. The ceiling was one of those textured ones that just looked gaudy and would be a pain in the ass to replace. My mind created various images, from animals to battles, out of the whorls and lines in the plaster—anything that prevented me from fixating on thoughts of my father.

It was odd being able to create images out of the texture. Texture itself wasn't a thing in Masas. Everything was sleek and smooth, honed into dangerously sharp edges. When I'd vowed to have the streets of Masas flow with blood, I'd ensured that any little thing around the kingdom could be used to accomplish that goal. Reflecting on it now, perhaps I overlooked the value of texture, especially on nights like tonight when my thoughts wouldn't stop running in damn circles.

I didn't want to admit to the fear I felt coursing through me. Fear that Ashera would somehow sever the mate bond because my spineless father was at the helm of this godsdamned rebellion. Fear that she would doubt my commitment to her... to us. Fear that she would think I'd slip back into my old ways of thinking, my old habits.

I continued to study the room around me, determined to strong-arm these thoughts into submission. I was no stranger to self-sabotage, and I wasn't about to let myself go down that path. I didn't even want to think about what the fae fuck would say if he learned any of this. That asshole would probably rub it in every chance he got, or worse... encourage Ashera to break the bond. I'd never heard of a bond being severed, but I knew better than to doubt my little queen. If she wanted something, she would damn well find a way to get it done. I suppressed a shudder before delicately extracting myself from the pile on the bed and shrugging on a pair of slacks.

I needed air.

The house Thorne owned spoke of his high rank within the former king's army. It was more of an estate than a house and easily took up a small block in its neighborhood. The house itself seemed to be U-shaped, based on what I'd been able to see out the window of our room, with an enclosed garden in the center. Despite being close to the heart of Zvida, it was far enough away from the palace to actually be backed by a forest, which made sense since the fucker was a shifter.

We hadn't stopped to explore the house, so I had no idea where anything was. I knew to get to the kitchen, I needed to go down the hall then down a flight of stairs. It would be at the end of that hall. Who the fuck knew what else there was in this place? It was reasonable to assume that there would be a way out from the kitchen. Slaves and servants were constantly coming and going, and the kitchen was the perfect place for all that hustle and bustle.

Easing the door closed behind me so as not to wake anyone else, I studied the hallway to ensure I wasn't about to run into any servants. Thankfully, the hall was blissfully empty. I moved slowly on the wooden floor, being careful to keep my steps light to prevent them from creaking. Most of the architecture seemed to lean toward natural wood textures, with accents of art thrown in. There was nothing that gave me any real insight to the shifter general, though, which was a shame. If he was really Ashera's mate, we needed to learn more about him. I wasn't about to just let anyone slide his cock into my mate's perfect little pussy.

I took my time getting to the kitchen. I didn't bother to explore, preferring to do that during the day, so instead I simply moved at a sedate pace to keep anything from making noise it otherwise wouldn't make. I wasn't in the mood for company, and this house was an unknown, so it was better to be cautious.

Once I finally made it to the kitchen, I stopped for a minute to look around. It was large enough to fit a small army, which didn't surprise me since Thorne was a shifter and those fuckers were huge. There was a large table in the center of the room made out of gleaming mahogany. There were scuffs and scars on the top, which suggested it was used fairly frequently. I was mildly curious if the general ate with his staff or if this was simply the servants' prep area. There was plenty of counter space. The old me wouldn't bother to ask him, but I was oddly curious.

Had Ashera shared meals with her servants before we'd come barging into her life? Would she want to associate with the palace staff? I'd seen how she was with her people at Beltane. No one had been beneath her. I wasn't even sure I really knew anything about my palace staff aside from their names. That had me wincing.

I hated what all of this said about Thorne. He was clearly well off, had obtained a very high rank within Qamar's military, and didn't seem as though he wanted for anything, yet he still seemed to socialize with his staff. He'd cared enough about them, about mortals, to defy and ultimately kill his king, all while I'd had my head shoved so far up my ass I couldn't see left from right. Gods, I'd been nothing but a self-centered asshole when I'd met Ashera. I'd fought my mate bond purely on the basis of not wanting to abolish slavery.

Thorne seemed to be everything I wasn't.

Fuck. I snarled quietly.

Finding a door on the other side of the kitchen, I was thrilled when I saw it led to the enclosed courtyard I'd spotted earlier through the bedroom window. I slipped out into the moonlit night, my chest heaving as I attempted to regain some semblance of control over my emotions. I was half tempted to wake Caspian so I could punch the fucker in the face. I had no doubt that would make me feel infinitely better.

I glanced around, trying to find something to take all of this energy out on. There was a large fountain in the middle of the courtyard. It had a sculpture of a dragon in the center with its neck arched up toward the sky and water spewing from its mouth. If I remembered correctly, dragons were the royal animal or some shit. The courtyard was lined with hedges that bloomed with brightly colored flowers, none of which I knew the names of, and the ground was covered with pavers to provide a smooth walking surface. This well-kept scenery only lasted up to the edge of the building itself. After that, there was a large expanse of lawn that abutted the forest. We'd be able to use the lawn for training, which was nice.

I made my way over to the fountain, still struggling not to let my fear get the best of me. Given how quickly I'd capitulated before she'd been kidnapped, I honestly wouldn't be surprised if she had doubts about me now. I ran my hand through my hair. She'd taken us all to task about being assholes, and I'd vowed to myself that I would spend each day demonstrating how genuine I was.

I couldn't pinpoint exactly when my thoughts on the matter started to change, and I admit that I'd originally only agreed to free Masas' slaves because I'd been desperate to get my cock inside my little queen, but after everything we'd been through, I could acknowledge that freeing slaves and giving women more power was the right thing to do. I could also acknowledge that I'd treated Masas' blood slaves abysmally. I would enact laws that protected anyone that wanted to donate blood. It wouldn't be easy, but it was possible.

"Why the fuck are you out of bed?" Malachi's voice set my teeth on edge. I needed one fucking minute to myself. One. Fucking. Minute.

"Not right now, Malachi." I tried, and failed, to keep the vicious snarl out of my voice.

"What crawled up your ass and died, princess?" The fucker decided to step up right next to me, bumping my shoulder with his. Of course he didn't feel like listening to me for once in his godsdamned life.

Was it too much to ask for a little fucking respect? Apparently.

"I'm going to say this one more time, Bat Fuck." I inhaled deeply. "Not right fucking now."

I didn't see the punch coming.

Light burst behind my eyes as my head snapped to the side from the force of the blow. That motherfucker. My fury lashed at my insides, causing my body to shake as I restrained myself from hitting him back. Killing Mal was a sure way to make Ashera break our mate bond.

"Come on, you fanged fuck. Hit me back." He shoved me.

"Fine."

I launched myself at him, toppling us both to the rough stone ground below. We landed a series of heavy blows, and soon the metallic scent of blood filled the air. I couldn't even say if I was landing more blows than I was blocking or if Malachi was landing more than I was. All I knew was that my arms and legs just kept flailing in his direction. Years of combat training flew out the window, replaced with a blinding fury that was fueled by my own insecurities and doubts.

Soft thuds echoed in the silence as we both attempted to aim for any body part we could reach. Every now and then, a muted groan would escape one of us. And yet... we were both holding back.

It irritated the fuck out of me that I didn't want to actually hurt the asshole. I just needed an outlet, and he'd happened to push my fucking buttons at just the right moment.

A well-timed punch from the incubus sent me rolling off him. My head landed against the ground with a thud, causing my ears to ring and stars to flash before my eyes. I groaned before turning my head to glare at Bat Fuck.

"Well, fuck you too!" I yelled as soon as the world stopped spinning.

Malachi kneeled next to me, wearing a stern expression on his face that had me wincing. "I know why you're out here." He pushed me back to the ground when I attempted to stand. "None of us think any less of you, Ambrose."

The affection in his voice surprised me. Yeah, we got along well enough, but none of us had really bothered to bond before. I refused to count that one time Fae Douche tried back in Masas. Nothing with him counted, because he was a shit stain. Mal and I had fucked, but it had all been to please Ashera. None of us were interested in touching anyone else unless she was around to enjoy the view.

"Ashera loves you," the demon continued, oblivious to my inner turmoil. "I've known her for hundreds of years. I've never seen her light up the way she does with you. Fuck, just seeing that mating mark on your chest has her gushing and feeling all dreamy. I'm surprised you haven't picked up on it through the bond."

I was too. Clearly, I'd been so stuck up my own ass that I hadn't realized just how strongly my mate felt about me. About all of us.

"We don't think you have anything to do with what's going on. Caspian might try to say otherwise, but he's a dumb fuck who needs to have his head caved in. Ashera, the one that really matters here, doesn't entertain that sort of nonsense. She fucking loves you, Ambrose."

My gaze finally met and held his, and a silent message passed between us. He'd beat me senseless to get his point across if he needed to. Strangely, it made me feel more secure.

Malachi was our de facto alpha of sorts.

He'd been with Ashera the longest and knew our mate better than she knew herself, so it had always been natural to listen to him, even if we didn't like it. He was now taking the time to tell me that I was being a dumb shit for doubting my bond with Ashera, for doubting myself and the rest of our merry band of assholes. Worse yet, for doubting Ashera.

Fuck. I don't want to have to owe him for this.

Pushing to my feet, I glowered at him as he slowly stood. Our eyes locked, and mine narrowed in challenge. The fucker punched me square in the nose.

"You're going to pay for that, Bat Fuck."

"Okay, Princess Ambrose." With that, he was gone, leaving me feeling far better than I had when I'd come out here. I didn't want to admit it, but the fucker had actually helped.

Ashera

I WAS STILL FLOATING in that wonderful hazy in-between where sleep meets the harsh reality of day, but an insistent tug on my nipple had my hands moving even though my eyes refused to open. Based on the texture of the hair as my palm ran along it and the head nuzzling against my breast, I knew it was Caspian. Calloused fingers slid up my stomach to glide over my neglected breast before tightly pinching my nipple.

My eyes flew open, and a startled yelp left my lips. My fae prince was grinning down at me with mischief sparkling in his ice-blue eyes. My own narrowed as I gazed up at him. He simply chuckled and went back to sucking on my nipple while his fingers tortured the other.

"Oh good, you woke her up." Malachi's deep timbre had heat flaring in my body. "I just finished kicking Ambrose's ass, so a good fuck with my little slut will be perfect."

Suddenly, my legs were spread and Mal's tongue ran teasing circles around my clit. My moan sounded frustrated and needy as one of my hands left Caspian's body to tangle in Malachi's hair, holding him in place. I arched my hips in an attempt to force my mate to pay proper attention to my aching bundle of nerves. My pussy fluttered, and I was painfully aware of just how empty I felt. My need ratcheted higher.

Caspian pulled away from my breast to watch as Malachi teased me, a vicious smirk spreading across his features. He grabbed my hands and pinned them over my head, causing me to curse violently under my breath.

"Now, now, Dick Slayer," Caspian scolded. "Let the assassin have his breakfast. He's not the only one who's starving for a taste of you."

Two large, blunt fingers slid deep into my pussy, instantly crooking to just the right angle to have my hips flying off the bed. Two more mouths latched onto my nipples—Ambrose and Jacobi. Where the hell had they come from? My thoughts scattered as Malachi started rubbing his fingers against my G-spot. He set a ruthless pace just as his lips sealed around my clit, and he sucked with the perfect amount of pressure.

My orgasm was quick and unexpected, and I shuddered with each pull of Mal's lips against my now sensitive flesh. Gods, it felt perfect. So fucking perfect.

Caspian adjusted himself next to me, his cock now level with my head. "I want you to choke on me, Dick Slayer."

"That's hard to do without a gag reflex," I teased.

He growled in response, adjusting his grip to hold my hands in one of his as his other tangled in my golden locks. I shot him a wink as I leaned in to lick the tip. He growled louder.

Malachi continued to feast on me as though I were the best meal he'd ever had, while my other two mates licked and nipped around my breasts, paying extra attention to my hardened buds. I moaned at the sensations flooding my body. None of them were applying enough pressure for me to be able to come again, which was perfect and agonizing at the same time.

I moaned as I wrapped my lips around Caspian's cock, marveling at the contrast between his delicious, chocolate colored skin and my own shimmering gold complexion. I loved how we looked as we came together—it was a secret pleasure of mine.

I worked Caspian at the same leisurely pace the others were working me. That didn't seem to please my fae prince, however, whose hand fisted tighter in my hair as he started to thrust down my throat. Every time he hit the back, I hummed, causing him to release a deep, pleasure filled groan.

"I said I wanted you to choke on my cock, Dick Slayer," Caspian growled, "so you're going to choke on my fucking cock."

He thrust into the back of my throat and held there. I swallowed around him, and he released a feral sounding snarl but stayed in place. I locked eyes with him as tears started to stream down my face. When I swallowed around him a second time, he pulled out.

"What a good fucking girl, Dick Slayer." I quirked a brow and smirked up at him.

With a burst of speed, my hands were released and all four of my mates were moving at the same time. I was left on my back on the bed as they rearranged themselves. Except... none of them moved over me. They were all sizing each other up, their stances defensive.

I propped myself up on my elbows and watched with increasing excitement. They only did this if they were going to fight over who was about to take a dick. The thought of one of my mates fucking each other... I moaned... perfect.

They moved in the blink of an eye—fists swinging, grunts ringing out, and bodies clashing. The fight didn't dampen my desire, no, it did the opposite. Need raged through every fiber of my being, leaving me panting as they continued to fight for dominance. I wanted to insert myself in the middle and lick all of them.

Then, just as suddenly as it started, they all stopped. Their chests heaved as they all gazed at one another before their heads all slowly turned toward me. I felt like prey in the best possible way.

Malachi cuffed Caspian by the back of the neck, his grip strong enough to cause the fae prince to wince. Jacobi mirrored the move with Ambrose. Oh? Was I about to get a show? My heart fluttered, and I struggled to pull in air as excitement screamed through me. I pushed myself into a sitting position, my eyes hungrily devouring each of my gorgeous mates as they all started to remove their clothes.

Come to mama. I wiggled my ass in excitement, purposely keeping myself from licking my lips and clapping my hands.

"Get on your hands and knees, little slut," Malachi commanded. "Make sure you're facing the end of the bed."

I hurried to comply, and my limbs seemed to flail at random in my eagerness to see what my mates had in store for me. The bed, while large, wasn't big enough to easily fit the five of us, but if we positioned ourselves appropriately, we should all be able to have sex.

Caspian slid carefully underneath me while Mal situated himself behind me. Jacobi and Ambrose approached the foot of the bed, with Jacobi holding with a bottle of lube in his hand.

There was a pregnant pause, one born of anticipation, pleasure, and promise. There was no room for jealousy here, only love and acceptance, and much to my pleasant surprise, we had started to find that and so much more over the last few days. I might have been worried before about all of my mates getting along, but I knew now, for certain, that the four males here with me would be just as committed to each other as they were to me. We were a family.

Malachi's fingers started to brush against my clit as Caspian's moved to toy with my nipples. "Don't look away from Jacobi and Ambrose, Sher. Watch what they do to each other."

Jacobi tossed the lube on the bed before reaching up to tangle both of his hands in Ambrose's hair, turning the vamp so they were facing each other. Gods, their cocks brushed. I was pretty sure I drooled. Mal kept playing with my clit, and Caspian continued with my nipples.

Jacobi pulled Ambrose flush against him before slanting his mouth over the vampire's. Ambrose growled low in his throat as his hands came up to tightly grip the angel's shoulders, their hips grinding together as they licked and sucked each other's mouths. One of Jacobi's hands wandered down Ambrose's back before his fingers dug into the toned flesh of the vamp's ass.

Ambrose groaned, rubbing his cock against Jacobi's again. He then ripped his mouth away and sank his fangs into the angel king's neck, which caused a ragged groan to fall from his lips. He didn't sip long before pulling away to slowly run his tongue over the wound, and Jacobi shuddered with pleasure.

Jacobi slid his hand around the front of Ambrose's body to curl his fingers around the cock rubbing against his own. He pumped the shaft a few times before getting to his knees in front of the vampire. He didn't waste any time sucking that cock into his mouth, and both men moaned at the feeling.

I'd been so absorbed watching two of my mates pleasure each other, I had almost forgotten about the two that were playing with my body. Malachi slapped my ass hard, the sting sending bolts of pleasure right to my clit. At the same time, Caspian eased the tip of his cock inside me, pumping with slow, lazy strokes designed to drive me wild.

Talk about the best possible sensory overload.

Ambrose threw his head back, thrusting his hips in time with Jacobi's mouth. I couldn't tear my gaze away even if my life depended on it. There was something about watching the way these two large, powerful men moved together that shook me to my core. All four of my mates were titans, and to see two of them locked passionately together as they each gave and received pleasure had my pussy fluttering around Caspian's cock and my heart soaring.

Caspian released a strangled groan, his hips jerking out of rhythm. Malachi kept torturing my clit, a dark chuckle rumbling from his chest.

"Do you like what you see, little slut?" His breath puffed against my back, causing me to arch in the hopes of feeling his lips against my skin.

I couldn't answer, too enraptured by the show and the feeling of my other two mates sliding against all the sensitive areas of my body. Was this paradise or was this torture? I wasn't sure. All I knew was that I didn't want any of them to stop.

Malachi fisted my hair, arching my back against his chest and causing Caspian to slide deliciously deeper into my pussy. My ragged moan told them how much I enjoyed the action.

"I asked you a question, little slut." He nipped my ear. "Do you like what you see?"

I attempted to nod, since I was beyond words at this point.

"Jacobi," Malachi barked. "Bring Ambrose over here."

My vampire's head snapped in our direction, a lethal glare marring his stunning face. Jacobi released Ambrose's cock with a pop before surging up and tightly gripping the nape of the vamp's neck. My angel king slammed the vampire prince forward so his chest was on the foot of the bed, grabbed the lube, and dribbled some over Ambrose's ass. He then rubbed some on his cock, his gaze finally lifting to lock with mine.

"Do you like what you see?" Malachi's harsh question, followed by the sting of his teeth against my neck, had me gasping and attempting to press myself further down on Caspian. I needed to move. It was too much, yet not nearly enough.

Jacobi slid one leg between Ambrose's and widened his stance, running his hand along the back of the vampire's thighs before rearing back for a brutal slap. It rang around the room, but Ambrose only moaned and buried his face in the blankets.

"One last time, little slut. Do you like what you see?"

Jacobi smirked at me in such a way that it was hard to believe he'd been chaste not too long ago. The angel in front of me looked and acted like a sexual master. I loved it.

"I love it," I bit out.

With that, Jacobi gripped Ambrose's hips and eased himself into the vampire, causing both men to release soft snarls of pleasure.

Caspian pulled my hips flush with his, while Malachi lined himself up and slid inside my pussy.

"Oh fuck!" I cried. I had never had both inside me like this before. The sting of the stretch felt so damn amazing. Both males grunted as Malachi slid his dick into the hilt, rubbing it against Caspian's along the way.

All of us froze, each taking deep inhales as we all adjusted.

"Move!" I commanded.

Thankfully, blissfully, they obeyed. Jacobi set a punishing pace inside Ambrose, but the vampire seemed to love every minute of the angel king fucking his ass. Meanwhile, Caspian and Malachi moved opposite each other, so there was also this delicious push and pull as their cocks rubbed together.

My back was still plastered against Mal's chest, so I allowed my head to drop to his shoulder, completely giving in to the pleasure.

"You two better fucking feed." Ambrose's muffled voice came from where his face was still pressed against the bedding.

He was right. We should eat.

Malachi and I both started to pull from the energy in the room. It was heady and made me feel as though I'd had one too many glasses of wine.

I watched as Jacobi wrapped his hand around Ambrose's cock, matching the stroke of his fist with his thrusts. Ambrose moaned louder, clenching the sheets in a death grip.

Mal lowered his hand and started to rub my clit, and my pussy clenched down viciously on both Caspian and Mal. They growled and began to move faster. I could feel the pleasure each of my mates was feeling in the bond.

Gods, it was too much.

We all shattered together, and my scream was drowned out by the roars released by my mates. We all collapsed in a satisfied pile, our limbs tangled and our breathing harsh as we recovered.

Several moments later, Malachi crawled his way out of bed, lifting me with ease as he went, and made his way over to the bathing room. He turned the shower on, waited for the water to heat up, and then walked us under the scorching stream.

My mate knew just how I liked my water—hot enough to boil my skin off.

My rock placed me on my feet, and I leaned back against him with a soft sigh. My other mates soon filed in, crowding the too small stall. No one complained, though, because we all wanted to be close.

Someone started to shampoo my hair, and I leaned into the touch.

Jacobi's soothing voice broke the silence. "We received an official summons from Qamar's new joint rulers. They want us to appear before them in court. They'd like to discuss our alliance."

We'd have to go out in public, which meant that I would need to remain in the shadows. I let out a small, disappointed sigh before I nodded. Just because we needed to do this didn't mean I had to like it. "Okay."

"We're meeting them at the summer palace, since we burned the main palace to the ground." Jacobi sounded amused.

It had been my small gift to Winta and Thorne. The thought of my two new mates had another pang hitting my chest. Soon, I'd need to sit down with these four and discuss bringing Winta and Thorne into the fold. All of them knew the importance of the mate bond, so I was hopeful they wouldn't give the two newcomers much of a hard time.

A thought struck me as I continued to ponder my newest mates— another queen. Two women in a sea of powerful men. I chuckled at the thought. Hopefully, the men would be able to keep up.

~

Jacobi

As we dressed for court, my thoughts turned toward Winta. Gods, how the times had changed, and all for the better in my opinion. It was thrilling watching Ashera navigate as a ruler, and I was sure the same would be said of watching Winta. Those two women had taken on men who were believed to be vastly more powerful than they were, and they won. Now, they were shining beacons for women everywhere, and beautifully deadly messages to men who sought to put them in their place.

Their place was on the throne with crowns on their heads. They were destined to shake things up, and I was extremely humbled I'd been chosen by Ashera to share her journey.

Gods, two strong women, two queens, now ruled two separate kingdoms in Dunya. It didn't matter that in the eyes of Dunya, Ashera was dead, we knew the truth.

I'd deemed these two kingdoms lesser than Malak. They'd owned slaves and treated their women poorly. Malak had always strived to be the pinnacle of morality, something for the other kingdoms to strive toward. Malak had never owned slaves and had always treated women with respect and dignity. We revered our women.

Yet... Malak had never seen a queen reign. I ruled while my older sister had been discarded. She should have rightfully ascended to the throne when Father died, and yet, it was never once questioned that I would become the next ruler.

I didn't know how to fix the guilt that weighed on me from a problem I hadn't started but had been complicit with. I cursed under my breath. I'd only helped to perpetuate views that women were lesser. *Fuck*.

There were two options for me to consider. The first, I could approach Eva and abdicate, allowing her the opportunity to lead should she wish to do so. The second, I could enact a law that enabled any firstborn child, regardless of sex, to assume the throne upon the death of the former ruler.

With regard to the first, would Eva even want to take the throne at this point? She seemed happy with her life. If she did agree to take the throne, would the people see her ascension as the forward progress I intended it to be? Or would they assume I was turning my back on them now that I was mated? Gods, how could I even turn to her now and tell her that she was to be the ruler from here on out? I'd certainly make myself available to her for anything and be there to assist as needed.

I'd made the foolish assumption that because she'd grown up with the belief that she was never going to inherit the throne, she didn't want it. Had she? I'd assumed she wanted the life she led. Gods, what if that was just a lie I told myself to feel better and cover the guilt because I knew it had been wrong for me to take the throne ahead of her? *Had* I known all along that there was something wrong with Malak's royal lineage? Had I simply turned a blind eye because we worshipped our women?

And what of the other women of Malak?

I ran my fingers through my hair in frustration. I'd opened a Pandora's box of problems—problems that I couldn't address right now. They would need to wait until we'd dealt with the resistance.

"Jacobi?" My mate's soft, sweet voice pulled me out of my thoughts. "What's bothering you?"

I glanced around, startled to find that we were no longer in Ashera's rooms at Thorne's house, but rather walking around what I assumed to be the summer palace. I'd been so consumed with my thoughts I hadn't taken notice of the journey here, which worried me more than I cared to admit. What if we had been attacked? Gods. Now was not the time to be stewing in my own mind, especially because Ashera was getting better at using her new powers, no doubt picking up on my foul mood not just through our bond, but through the use of her angelic abilities. That was also another issue that needed to be dealt with at a later time.

She was now standing next to me, tugging lightly on my hand and forcing me to look down at her. She was dressed in her training leathers and a lightweight black cloak with a deep hood that covered her face. My queen was making sacrifices for a better world, and I would happily sacrifice right along with her.

When I'd first arrived in Shaytan, I hadn't realized that Ashera would be such a visionary. She'd left the capital city basically untouched. The streets all led to the palace, with rows of houses built in circles that spiraled away from the monolithic structure in the center. The former king had wanted to make a statement with his capital city, casting much of it in gold and jewels. Frankly, it was hideous to look at, and when I'd arrived to see that not much had changed, my heart had sunk a bit.

But now... Now I knew things hadn't physically changed around the palace of Shaytan, but they'd changed drastically inside. The appearance of the country would slowly morph as time progressed. Ashera had shown me so much in the short time we'd been together. I was more grateful than she could ever possibly realize.

"Jacobi?" She tugged on my hand again, snapping me once more out of my thoughts.

"Yes, my love?" Her brow furrowed in concern as she stared up at me. The only features I could clearly make out under her hood were her stunning emerald green eyes.

I knew she could feel my tumultuous emotions. I also knew that I needed to keep a tighter rein on them now that Ashera was coming into her new abilities. She had enough to deal with and did not need to add my own inner conflict to the list, especially when I wasn't sure how to go about fixing the issue at the moment.

I gave her a gentle smile and squeezed her hand before brushing my fingers over her cheek. "It's nothing, my love. I'm just tired. I didn't get much sleep last night."

Ashera's emerald eyes narrowed, a suspicious glimmer sparking to life inside her gaze. It was clear that she didn't believe a single word I said. Thankfully, I knew she wouldn't push the topic, not while we were in mixed company, strolling the elaborate summer estate Winta had decided to hold court in.

The estate reminded me of the nobles' houses in Malak. It was made out of stark white bricks that rose to a staggering four stories. The roof was made out of clay tiles and had several chimneys sticking out of it. The front garden boasted a hedge maze with a large marble fountain jutting out of its center, and there were several stone benches scattered around the outer edge of the maze.

The paths around the palace were made from crushed stones and lined with colorful blooming flowers. We were outside of Zvida, deep in the woods. Surprisingly, the sounds of wildlife filled the air. I would have assumed with all the shifters around, prey animals would keep clear of the palace. Interesting. I'd have to ask Winta or Thorne about that later. The air out here was cleaner too, less congested.

While it had been immensely satisfying to watch the palace in Zvida burn to the ground, that act had subsequently raised a few logistical issues. Winta and Thorne needed to weed through the nobles who had remained after Vaughn's beheading to determine how well they would fit within the new regime. They would also need to appoint new nobles, hold court, and do all of the other boring administrative tasks that came with running a kingdom.

While we certainly could have run things out of Thorne's home—it was roughly the size of a small castle—with Ashera staying there, it wasn't wise to also have a flood of people coming and going. Thankfully, Winta had said that she'd grown up mostly in the summer palace, and while it was a bit outside of the city, it would be more than adequate to suit their current needs. She hadn't disclosed why she'd grown up in the palace, which was something we would bring up with her at today's meeting.

I assumed that she wouldn't want to hide anything from Ashera since they were mates, but we didn't know much about either of the joint rulers, and until we did, we needed to be cautious. There had been too many attempts on her life, and none of us wanted to go through another.

"I think we're all aware of your lack of sleep, birdbrain. All any of us could hear was you screwing Dick Slayer's brains out when you thought the rest of us were sleeping." Caspian huffed a laugh and punched me in the shoulder as he passed.

Heat rushed to my cheeks. I'd certainly thought they were all asleep when I had turned to Ashera last night. I'd been half crazed for her, needing to feel her wet heat gripping my cock as I thrust into her. The way she came apart in my arms made me feel far more powerful than I ever thought I could be. The fact that this powerful woman, a queen, would sob for my cock, come undone around me, and lose herself in me... it was a gift beyond measure.

Ashera whipped her head around and glared at the fae prince. "Watch yourself, Cas," she reprimanded him sharply before giving me a sweet smile.

"Thank you." I placed a reverent kiss on her brow. "Did you feed enough?" Even though Qamar was technically our ally, I wanted to make sure Ashera remained full and ready to take on anything that might come our way, especially when I closed my eyes and saw her dying all over again almost every night. I'd do everything in my power to ensure that never happened again.

"Of course!" Ashera held my hand, preventing me from continuing on with the others down the path that led to the palace's entrance. "Jacobi..."

"My love, I assure you, I am fine." I cradled her face in my hands and leaned down to kiss her delicious lips. I loved this female more than life itself.

Malachi stopped outside of a large set of double doors and spoke with a shirtless guard. The man was massive, almost taller than Malachi—who was at least seven feet tall—with broad shoulders that explained the need for the enormous doors I'd seen all throughout the kingdom. It seemed that shifters were averse to most articles of clothing, with many of the males choosing to wear leather pants and nothing else. Though I supposed that made sense if they ever needed to shift in a hurry.

Did all of the guards have to be created with bulging six-packs and biceps the size of my head? I wasn't a small male by any stretch of the word, and neither was Malachi, but some of these shifters made me feel like nothing more than a child. Gods, if I wasn't secure in my mating with Ashera, I'd probably be in their faces the same way Ambrose was with Thorne.

I shook my head and studied the doors we now stood in front of as Malachi continued to talk with the guard. They were a bronzed gold and intricately carved with three panels apiece. Each section illustrated a glorious battle. The first displayed a heavily muscled jaguar ripping out the throat of another feline animal. The second depicted a war eagle, covered in armor, swooping toward a castle, its beak open in a battle cry. The final panel was of a dragon, breathing fire and facing a whole army on its own. I wondered if these were like the tapestries we'd seen in Masas. Did they demonstrate the royal family's rise to power? Their greatest triumphs?

The scenes on the doors certainly had to be ancient. Dragons were a dying breed, and as far as I knew, the last one had been King Vaughn. At least that was what the rumors said. Hundreds of years before I'd been born, nobles and royals from the other kingdoms had begun to collect dragon shifters as pets or trophies. The more dragons one had, the more powerful you were thought to be. Taming a dragon was believed to be the highest achievement one could ever make. The rationale had been to demonstrate how strong you truly were through the capture and control of a feral dragon.

Dragons hadn't taken to captivity. Most never bred, and those who did gave birth to young who died within moments of leaving the womb, so their numbers had slowly dwindled. I hadn't seen one myself in centuries, not since I was a child.

I'd been on a diplomatic mission with my father to Sahira, and had witnessed a small, extremely malnourished dragon curled around the king's throne. At first, I hadn't been sure what the creature was, but it had lifted its reptilian head and looked right at me. I'd asked my father about it, and he'd silenced me and told me that such barbaric practices weren't followed in Malak, but we weren't to question the way other kingdoms were ruled. Perhaps I should have known then that Malak would be different than other kingdoms, but we were certainly complicit in keeping slaves and women as second-class citizens.

I glanced over at Ashera, who was also studying the doors to the summer palace. Her mating mark for Visa was a dragon, but I don't recall Ashera ever saying that her mate had been a dragon shifter. Our marks typically represented an aspect of ourselves, but that certainly didn't mean Visa had been a dragon.

Done chatting with the guard, Malachi turned to face us. "Everyone ready?"

Ambrose scoffed as if he was offended by the question. "We've met the rulers before, this isn't exactly a big deal."

Mal leveled Ambrose with a look similar to one a parent would give a child who was clearly being a brat. "Yes, but now we're meeting them in an official capacity as representatives of our individual kingdoms. This will be the first time Winta and Thorne will be formally accepting us as allies. It will also be our opportunity to recognize the legitimacy of their reign." The incubus rolled his eyes.

Ashera interrupted all of us by sharply clearing her throat, and all heads turned in her direction. She let go of my hand so she could turn to each of her mates with a death glare and determination shining in her eyes. "This is an important day for Winta and Thorne. I was in Winta's position not too long ago. You will each show her the respect she deserves. You will also recognize her as an equal joint ruler next to Thorne. Am I clear?"

We all gave her a sedate nod of our heads.

"Then we can celebrate with them before heading back to our rooms to plan what to do next. We're barely keeping ahead of the rebellion, and we need to reassess our options, not to mention everything else that's going on."

We all nodded again.

"So we're going to discuss the rebellion that wants your head on a silver platter, two shifters claiming you as their mate, and the nice new powers you're displaying?" Malachi raised a dark brow at her. "I just want to make sure we're clear on the agenda."

Ashera glared at him before shrugging her shoulders. "Yes."

Malachi chuckled and shook his head before ushering us through the doors and into the summer palace.

2

ASHERA

I hadn't been able to speak to Thorne or Winta before they'd left Thorne's house that morning. It was possible that my little dalliance with my mates caused me to run a bit late. Maybe. But I was well aware that adding two more mates to the mix would shake up our dynamic, and each of my current mates would need reassurance that no matter what happened, I loved each of them, so it was important that we'd had that time together this morning.

What bothered me, however, was knowing that I hadn't sought out Thorne or Winta prior to this. I'd barely spoken more than a handful of words to either of them. The thought made me wince. They were my mates, and I hadn't bothered to try to get to know them. I'd need to rectify the issue, especially if we wanted to finalize the bond.

As we made our way down the large, overly ornate entrance hall, I made sure to keep to the shadows as much as possible. It wasn't hard, since there were statues and pillars everywhere to hide behind. The white brick that made up the facade of the building continued through to the entrance hall, the polished stone lining the walls. Every few feet or so, a chandelier hung from the ceiling, decked out in gold and crystals. The rug on the floor was so plush, my feet sank with each step. Every inch of the space screamed opulence and luxury.

It was still better than the gaudy as fuck main palace.

I watched my mates move with confidence and grace, each a perfectly lethal weapon wrapped in delicious velvet flesh. Gods, a confident male was such a turn-on. I had to check and make sure that I hadn't started drooling.

Their lethal grace made me so proud that I'd decided to make them all kings in their own right. I knew Mal loathed the thought of being king, we'd discussed it during our early planning of the coup in Shaytan. He'd told me there was no way he'd ever want to be king, so knowing that he was the acting king now tickled me to no end.

I'd surprised my four established mates when I'd announced I'd been in the process of appointing them all as kings of Shaytan. We hadn't finalized how we wanted Dunya to look now that we'd mated, and I knew we would have to do that sooner rather than later. It certainly didn't make things easier knowing that I was technically dead and couldn't actually make any proclamations. We would have to navigate all of this as cautiously as possible.

All seven of us—Winta and Thorne included—needed to sit down after today to cement a better strategy for moving forward. There were still so many things we needed to tackle. We needed to find Ambrose's father and most likely kill him, which meant we had to figure out how to ensure a peaceful transfer of power within Masas. We couldn't be fighting several wars in several different kingdoms.

We also needed to ascertain the state of Sahira. I was concerned that we hadn't heard from King Judah. There had been witches in Masas, but that didn't necessarily mean that Sahira was directly involved with the resistance. While we couldn't rule it out, we shouldn't make assumptions either. The most pressing question was whether King Judah was working with Tomas. Had the witch king been working with Tomas this entire time? And was he now giving the vampire sanctuary?

If we didn't plan this out correctly, we could end up starting several civil wars alongside the war against the resistance. Dunya wasn't prepared for violence on that scale. The current supply chains wouldn't be able to handle it, especially since Shaytan had abolished slavery. We were still figuring out how to appropriately distribute Shaytan's resources.

I sighed in frustration and tugged on the edges of my hood to better cover my face. There was no use thinking about things now. It had to be a group discussion, especially considering the possibility of impending violence. Gods, this could all backfire horribly and kill my mates.

That thought sent panic racing down my spine, and pain lanced my heart. I wouldn't lose another mate. Never again.

"Sher?" Malachi's warm hand slid onto my lower back, pulling me out of my thoughts. I'd been so caught up in my head I hadn't noticed him hanging back. "Come on, Ashera. Talk to me."

I sighed again as I studied his face. I loved his deep olive skin, honey colored eyes, and large, lethal horns. He was my rock, my best friend, and anything else I might need him to be. The love I had for him hurt sometimes in its intensity, but I always basked in its glow.

"So much could go wrong, Mal. Just one mistake could kill all of you." My voice was a soft, broken whisper.

He knew, better than the others, what losing Visa had done to me. His gaze locked with mine before he leaned down to gently press his forehead to mine. A fierce wave of love and devotion came from him as we both closed our eyes for a moment.

"Nothing is going to take us from you, Sher. I won't let it," he vowed.

I tangled my fingers with his, desperate to keep us connected. "I wouldn't make it through that again."

"You won't need to, my queen." Malachi untangled his fingers from mine so he could cup my cheeks, his thumbs stroking against my skin. "We won't leave you."

I allowed myself one more moment with Mal before I pulled away from him. It wouldn't do to have him show such affection to someone who wasn't his mate, since I was still dead. His eyes shone with love, and I could feel his dedication, adoration, loyalty, and passion with my new powers. He was just as lost to me as I was to him. I gave him a wobbly smile and a nod to let him know we needed to keep moving.

I waited until he'd gone into the throne room before shuffling in and keeping to the back of the space. Just as the main palace's throne room had been, this chamber was far more opulent than the throne room in Shaytan, and I'd thought that had been hideous and gaudy. Every inch of the space was covered in gold, silver, and precious gemstones. The ceiling was painted in gems and dripped with crystal chandeliers, and the floor was made of marble with gold veins running through the stone. It was shaped like a rectangle, with the large double doors on one end and the thrones, raised several feet off the main floor, on the other. The longer walls were adorned with portraits of who I presumed were the previous rulers of Qamar. The vast majority of them had a large male dominating the center, a female tucked into his side, and a large dragon soaring in the background. My eyes narrowed as I looked at the portraits. The women were made to look much smaller and appeared scared and weak. I rolled my eyes.

All four of my mates approached Winta and Thorne, who were seated on subtle thrones made of what appeared to be an opal-like stone. The two were dressed in leathers that were embroidered and beaded to look beautiful, but they were still clearly functional as a form of protection as well. Smart. They wore small crowns made of gold that reminded me of my circlet back in Shaytan.

Qamar's nobles were scattered throughout the room, each dressed in finery more over the top than necessary. I assumed this was the standard when King Vaughn held court. I wouldn't be surprised if Winta and Thorne made things a little more casual. The shifters, in general, didn't seem quite as stuffy as the other species. Perhaps it had something to do with the fact that they shared their soul with a wild animal. Regardless of the reason, I liked it.

I made the decision to open up my new empathic gifts to determine if any of the nobles meant to undermine the new ruling pair. I was sure Jacobi was doing the same, but I needed the practice. I could also study everyone in the room in a way Jacobi couldn't right now because his attention needed to be on Winta and Thorne. I took a deep breath to brace myself for the onslaught of emotions before relaxing my mental walls.

It was overwhelming for a moment, akin to standing in a crowded room where everyone was screaming at the top of their lungs, except there were no words and the feelings would suddenly cut off altogether. A dull ache started in the back of my head as I attempted to decipher each emotion and determine where that feeling was coming from.

I decided to focus on Malachi first. I knew how he was feeling and recognized the cadence of his emotions. I let everything else fade into the background. From there, I focused on each of my other mates, Winta and Thorne included. I found if I looked at the person, it was much easier to separate their emotions from the rest of the crowd. I'd need to work on that, but it helped for the time being.

As I went through the nobles in the room, my mates went through the traditional introductions and presentations. It was all so horribly boring, and I was glad I didn't have to deal with it myself. Waiting to be introduced to someone had to be my least favorite aspect of being queen. I'd done away with the tradition in Shaytan because we wouldn't have been able to get anything done otherwise. They'd be a while, so this gave me plenty of time to learn as much as I could while hiding in the shadows.

All of the nobles seemed to feel fairly neutral at the moment, and none of them were impatient to leave. Some felt mildly curious about my mates, while others were hungry, but none seemed to be harboring any ill intent, at least at the moment. I wouldn't forget the feelings of animosity that had rolled through the crowd when King Vaughn had been beheaded. I had no way of telling if those emotions had belonged to anyone in this room. I'd have to stay alert. I hoped that most ran off to the resistance and hadn't hung around to cause chaos.

"Your Majesties." I almost choked when Caspian spoke first. My hostile fae was going to pretend to be a decent male? I had to see this. "We have come before you to offer an alliance with the Kingdoms of Shaytan, Malak, and Masas."

We'd discussed this beforehand. Since Ambrose had been acting in Tomas's stead, and no one knew any different, we'd keep to the status quo. As far as the rest of Dunya was concerned, he was still the acting ruler for Masas, which played in our favor since that gave him the authority to enter into alliances with other kingdoms.

It was only a matter of time before we officially deposed Tomas anyway. He was one of our top priorities now that Winta and Thorne were rulers of Qamar. We'd talked briefly about heading back to Masas, but nothing had been decided yet. It could be beneficial for Ambrose to seize power there rather than killing his father and lugging his severed head back to Masas.

Caspian, on the other hand, couldn't enter into alliances on his own. His father was still very much King of Juniya. As far as we knew, he hadn't taken a stance in regard to the rebellion. That meant Juniya would need to stay out of this alliance for the time being, until Caspian could confer with his father. Determining Juniya's stance in all of this was yet another thing we needed to tackle. Caspian was sure that if his father wasn't actively involved in the resistance, he was at least complicit, which meant there was the potential for yet another civil war.

I was so damn tired of fighting. Was it too much to ask for peace? Just for a minute?

The nobles' interest spiked, pulling my attention back to my mates. We weren't sure how many people knew that Tomas had been staying in Qamar's palace when Winta and Thorne enacted their coup, but it seemed that more than a few knew or suspected something was going on. Their interest was directed entirely at Ambrose.

It wasn't public knowledge that Tomas was part of the resistance, but the nobles that knew he'd been here were starting to feel far more curious than I was comfortable with. None of them felt duplicitous... yet. I didn't know any of them, so I didn't trust any of them. I'd have to tell Winta and Thorne to have their nobles watched for a few days to see if any of them did anything that might raise red flags.

Winta and Thorne both grinned down at my mates before Winta rose and held out her hands. "We are so pleased to receive you all officially. Welcome to Qamar, friends."

Thorne got to his feet beside her. "We are so very excited to open negotiations between our great kingdoms. Qamar readily accepts your offers of an alliance." He, too, held out his hands toward my mates. "We are most pleased that the mates of Queen Ashera, may she rest in peace, have come to offer us an alliance. We relish the chance to assist you as you hunt down those who would seek to destroy freedom."

They both stepped down to stand directly in front of my men, and

Winta's husky voice carried around the room. "Let us retire to my office. We have delicate matters of state to discuss." To the rest of those gathered, she said, "Please feel free to retire to the rooms that have been prepared for you. We will ensure your every need is taken care of."

We all filed out of the throne room. Two guards larger than Malachi—which just boggled my mind—walked behind me as we made our way down a series of halls. I tried to keep track of where we were going, but it was a maze of turns. I was surprised we didn't end up walking right back into the throne room.

The office we entered was ornate, yet homey. It was clearly a well used space, much like the study in my palace. All the walls were lined with floor to ceiling bookshelves, except for the opposite wall, which had large windows with a stunning view of the forest that sprawled behind the palace. What looked like a lone, small mountain rose in the distance. It was extremely peaceful.

There was a round fireplace in the center of the room and two desks on either side of it, both piled high with papers and books. My lips quirked as I noted how disheveled everything seemed. Having spent centuries cleaning, I loved when things got a bit messy, especially my men.

Everyone fanned out around the room. The two guards remained in the hallway, leaving the seven of us alone. I flicked my hood from my face and removed my cloak. Both Thorne and Winta stepped up to me, their lips breaking into stunning smiles.

Thorne, his chocolate brown eyes shimmering with mischief and heat, looked positively delicious packed into his ceremonial leathers. His wide shoulders, large biceps, and six-pack were clearly defined as though the leather had been painted on. I subtly clenched my lips closed to make sure that I wasn't drooling. His rich tan skin, not quite as dark as Caspian's or Winta's, would look amazing draped over mine. He had a hint of a five o'clock shadow gracing his strong, defined chin.

Winta, in contrast, while still tall—taller than me—only came up to Thorne's shoulders. She looked just as delicious in her skintight leathers as Thorne did. Her braided hair was woven in intricate patterns around her head, and I realized I could spend hours getting lost in her dark eyes. She was leaner than I was, not as curvy, but I could still see hints of soft breasts and rounded hips, and like the other shifter women I'd seen around Qamar, she was built with muscle, all lethal grace.

"Mate," they rumbled in unison, causing my lips to quirk.

"I'm happy to see that you made it here safely." Winta's gaze was soft and gentle as she took me in. Thorne nodded his agreement, his own eyes fiery as they trailed over my body. Both gazes caused tingles of awareness to flutter through my veins, and I had to remind myself that now was certainly not the time to finalize my bonds with these two.

"This isn't the first time I've had to hide my identity, though I do hope it is the last." The four males on the other side of the room growled their agreement, and I shot them a soothing look. We all knew this was temporary.

"I noticed the dragons adorning your doors on the way in," Jacobi mentioned, drawing everyone's attention to him.

"And the dragons in the portraits in the throne room," I added. Jacobi and I grinned at each other.

"The entire royal family are dragon shifters." Winta smiled. "I have a few cousins living in the southern cave systems and throughout various mountain ranges in Dunya."

"Wait." I held up my hand and studied Winta. "You're a member of the royal family?"

Winta nodded. "We deposed my father."

"Holy fuck," Caspian muttered.

"The fucker had it coming. I warned him this would happen, but he ignored me. It just goes to show that men really do think with the smaller of their two heads," Winta scoffed and shook her head.

I snorted. That was such a Visa thing to say. I paused. She'd actually said that same phrase numerous times during her life. Malachi's eyes met mine and held.

"Visa." I sighed and we shared a bittersweet smile. I'd been thinking about her more lately, especially since coming to Qamar. She'd have been so proud of the work we'd been able to accomplish thus far. She'd also have gone off on her own and tried to light the whole resistance on fire. She hadn't been a particularly strong succubus, but she'd fought like a wild thing and had such a fiery temper.

Sometimes I'd work her up on purpose because she always loved as hard as she fought. She'd been glorious. She'd been mine.

"How do you know my dragon's name?" Winta's question, asked so softly, stopped my heart.

My gaze flew back to her, searching for something I couldn't name. My pulse pounded loudly in my ears, and my breathing grew rapid. Her dragon... Its name was Visa? I... I couldn't process this. All I could focus on was Visa's name running on repeat in my head. How... How could this be? There was no possible way this could be a coincidence. Gods. I could feel my hands start to tremble as the backs of my eyes began to burn.

Malachi's hand landed on my shoulder, and he squeezed it gently while my other mates clustered around us.

"Your dragon's name is Visa?" he asked. I was grateful he said something. There was no way I was going to be able to speak right now, not without crying.

"Yes." Her gaze bounced between the two of us, a question clear in her eyes. "What's going on?"

"My—" My voice broke, and I coughed. "My first mate's name was Visa."

Silence reigned heavily in the room. All eyes were glued to me. Malachi, Ambrose, Caspian, and Jacobi all radiated concern and love. Thorne and Winta felt those things as well, but they also felt intrigued, especially Winta. My heart felt as though it was about to take flight from my chest. I blinked back tears, glancing up at the ceiling in an attempt to dry my eyes. I could now feel Winta's confusion and an echo of the heartache I felt.

Our gazes locked. Held.

One heartbeat went by. Two.

My fangs dropped of their own accord, and I stepped into Winta. Her hands gripped my hips. My instincts had taken over, fueled by my urge to claim Winta as my mate as well as the heartache of losing Visa. Something in my newest mate called to me in a way that the others hadn't. The urge to sink my fangs into her and taste her blood was overwhelming. It was all I could focus on.

I took one long drag of Winta's scent. Visa had smelled like this, like home. I sank my fangs into her neck.

～

"Come on then, you fiery beast," I called in a laugh as I ran, naked, for the shore of the pond that bordered our small cottage. "You said you would go for a swim with me."

"That was before you had a meeting with Malachi without me." Visa snorted, just as naked as I was, as she tore down the grass path, matching me stride for stride. Her long, dark hair flowed behind her in waves as she ran, and her eyes, which were a soft violet, would darken or lighten depending on her mood. Right now, they were a soft lavender that sparkled with joy. She had skin that was paler than mine, smooth and unblemished. I loved leaving hickeys all over her body. We were roughly the same height, which was perfect for leaning in at random to kiss her.

"Well, it's not my fault you went to work!" I couldn't contain my laughter as she tripped on her own feet and went catapulting into the pond. The water quickly concealed her body from view.

I dove in after her, eager to spend time with my mate. We'd both been so busy between work and the coup that we hadn't spent much time alone together. We needed this. We both surfaced with a laugh, our bodies brushing. The fire I felt for her flared brightly, and I lightly trailed my fingers from her hips to the underside of her breasts. Visa always took my damn breath away. Her skin was so soft and warm.

"Can you forgive me?" I asked with a pout, gently flicking her nipples. I wanted to watch her unravel and hear her cries of passion as she came. Visa was so beautiful when she came for me.

"You think you can distract me with sex?" Her smirk had me biting back one of my own. "You can try."

"Come now." I pulled her closer and licked her red lips. "Don't be mad. You know we're just planning, and besides, I always tell you everything we discuss."

Visa leaned in to nip my lips. "I know, love."

Her lips, so soft and full, pressed lovingly against mine. Our tongues tangled as her hands weaved into my hair, pulling us together. I slid my hands to her hips, happily holding her to me as we kissed.

I could kiss this woman forever.

She pulled back. "I love you more than I could ever say, Ashera. The gods truly blessed me when they made you my mate."

My heart stuttered. "I feel the same, Visa. Always."

~

THE SOUND *of galloping horses had me quickening my pace. It was odd to hear the sound so close to my cottage. I was coming home from another meeting with Malachi. We had much of the Shaytanian army on our side, and I couldn't wait to share the news with Visa. She'd told me to go without her today, wanting to go to the market and run other errands. We needed to maintain our normal lives so as not to arouse suspicion.*

Three horsemen rushed past me, all incubus lords, not paying any mind to the cloaked figure walking on the street. My heart rate spiked at the sight, and my stomach churned violently. My mind turned as I raced home. I searched my bond, almost collapsing when I felt Visa was still alive, but my relief was short-lived as my cottage came into view.

A frantic yell ripped from my chest. The door had been torn from its hinges, the windows shattered, and a fire had been lit on the thatched roof. There was no sign of my mate outside.

"Visa!" My scream echoed around me. "Visa! Answer me!"

I... I couldn't feel her. She was still alive, but I couldn't feel anything else down our bond. Panic rising, I ran into the burning cottage. My eyes watered almost instantly as I began to search our destroyed home.

Whoever had done this—and I suspected the lords were responsible—had ripped and shredded everything. Nothing seemed to be spared.

I coughed and covered my nose and mouth with the edges of my cloak, fighting to find my mate through the tears running down my face. The loud rhythm of my heart roared louder than the flames. I shifted through debris, my fingers bleeding as I blindly dug through the ruins.

"Visa! Gods, Visa! Please!" My throat felt raw, and I coughed again. "Visa!"

My foot connected with something soft, and I dropped to my knees, searching with my hands. Warm flesh met my fingers, and I let out a sob of relief. I found her. Thank the gods.

Gripping whatever my fingers came into contact with, I pulled her, inch by excruciating inch, from our burning cottage, stopping only once I felt the gentle lap of water from the lake.

I quickly removed my cloak, turned to gulp down the cool water, and scrubbed the tears from my eyes, then I turned back to my mate.

My breathing stopped, and my heart plummeted. I distantly recognized the sound of screaming.

My knees gave out, and all I could do was stare at what was left of my mate. How she could possibly still be alive was a mystery.

Visa was naked. Her flesh had all been removed and her bones broken. They'd extracted her eyes as well as her tongue, based on the bleeding coming from her mouth. They'd ripped her open, leaving her uterus hanging from her body. I turned and gagged, trying to keep my food in my stomach and failing.

I gently took her into my arms and rested her head on my thighs. I could still hear the screams, but I didn't bother trying to see who it was. All I could focus on was my mate. My Visa.

Gods.

Her breath shook her chest, each one growing weaker. I was losing her. No. No, no, no, no, no. I started rocking, careful not to jar her in any way. My mind shrieked "no" on repeat. Not like this.

"Visa, my love," I whispered, my voice hoarse. The screaming had stopped when I started to speak. "I am so, so sorry I wasn't here to protect you."

My hands trembled as they found their way to one of the daggers secured to my thigh. It took several tries before I could slip it from its holster. I couldn't let her continue to suffer. Not like this.

The screaming was back again. Gods! I wished it would just stop!

Without moving my precious, beautiful mate, I gripped the dagger in both hands.

"I love you. I will follow you on to the next world after I see the ones who did this to you pay. I promise, Visa. They will all die worse deaths." With that, I slammed my blade into her heart.

The screaming never stopped.

≈

SEEING Visa's head mounted in the king's throne room, front and center like some sort of trophy, snapped something inside me. He'd dug up my mate, placed a preservation spell on her, and displayed her for all to see.

I bathed in all of their blood that night, coated my skin with it until there was nothing left of me. I'd become a beast of vengeance.

~

I PULLED BACK, my fangs dripping Winta's blood down my chest as we stared at one another in shock. Based on the expression on her face, she'd seen everything I had. She'd lived my memories with me. My heart trembled with the realization that my mate, my Visa, was standing here in front of me. She'd been reborn, and her soul was just as stunning as it had been in her former life.

"Ashera." Her voice broke as tears streamed from her eyes. Winta was just as overcome as I was. Her emotions flashed too rapidly for me to make sense of them, but I had a feeling they were similar to mine.

The dragon mark on my arm burned.

"Winta." My voice broke, too, as I realized what that burning sensation meant. I raised my shaking hands to gently hold her face. How hadn't I seen it before? "You..."

"You saved me." My eyes widened with shock. "Your love. It saved me. Instead of moving into some vacant afterlife... I was reborn. Your love, our bond, was my tether."

"Winta." Her name left my lips on a sob. My heart simultaneously shattered and repaired itself as her words sank in. I'd brought her back to me. Our bond had conquered death.

Winta crushed her lips to mine, framing my face with her hands as I tangled my fingers between her braids. Our tongues met, retreated, and met again. A desperate hunger, one born of loss and reunion, ripped through us both. Our breaths left us in shaky exhales as our bodies came together.

"I will never let you go again," I whispered when our lips parted. "Never again."

"Never," she agreed.

I stepped into her, pressing my body flush to hers. I needed to feel her against me, needed to reaffirm the bond I'd thought long dead. I needed to hear her breathe. I needed all of her. Right now.

Spinning us so I could press Winta into the door, I made quick work of removing my mate's clothes. The need to feel my fingertips glide along her flesh was so strong it had me ripping the offending items more than actually removing them.

Winta was not Visa, but they shared a soul—a soul so stunningly beautiful it brought tears to my eyes. I thought I'd never be able to bask in its glow again. I was so humbled the gods saw fit to bless me with it once more.

My hands shook as I caressed every inch of her body I could touch. Our lips met again and again, leaving little nibbles and teasing licks. This lovemaking was different than with my other mates. I wanted time to savor her, but the urge to solidify our bond once again pushed me to move faster.

I could take my time devouring my luscious mate later.

Trailing kisses down Winta's neck, I plucked her nipples, teasing the taut peaks until a quiet whimper left my mate's lips, her back arching into my touch. I smirked against her collarbone when her hands tangled in my hair and tried to push me farther south.

She was always so desperate for me to get to the end. She hadn't changed.

I nipped at the valley between her breasts before soothing the sting with my tongue. My fingers abandoned her nipples in favor of traveling south, and I replaced them with my mouth.

She tasted just as Visa always had, of freshly cleaned laundry and the forest right after a thunderstorm. It sent my senses reeling, and I bit back a moan. Her pleasure was my main focus right now. I could drown myself in her taste once our bond was more secure and my shock had worn off.

"Ashera." Her breathy moan made me grin against her breast.

I trailed my fingers down the front of her thighs, lightly scratching against her soft, chocolate brown skin. Her legs widened, followed by the soft thunk of her head falling back against the door. She tugged on my head again, a clear demand for me to kneel before my queen—a decree I was all too happy to obey.

My knees silently met the floor, and the only sounds that registered were Winta's breathy pants as I scraped my nails up her inner thighs. I trailed my mouth down her stomach, leaving small nips and playful licks along the way.

Every touch, every kiss, left me feeling drunk and dizzy from the sight, scent, smell, and taste of her. I locked gazes with her as she looked down her body at me. We shared a small smile before I started to stroke my fingers along the seam of her soaked folds. A dark chuckle escaped my lips as I leaned in, swirling my fingers around Winta's clit and teasing her by not making contact.

"Ashera." She tugged at my golden locks, and I chuckled again. I supposed I was being mean. We'd waited all this time to be together again.

I closed my mouth on her clit as my fingers sank into her velvety warm heat, and we both groaned at the sensation. I curled my fingers to ensure I hit her G-spot with each thrust as I slid my tongue over her.

"Oh gods, yes. Ashera, yes!" Her cries spurred me on, and I increased the pace of my fingers and the pressure of my mouth against her clit.

Winta's hips bucked against my face. I leaned away from her clit for a moment and ordered, "Play with your nipples, Queen," and then I instantly returned to worshipping her.

I soaked in the vision of a flushed Winta with her fingers plucking at her nipples, her hips bucking and thighs twitching as I continued my assault on her body. She chanted my name, and my pleasure rose with hers. I'd always been able to orgasm with Visa, even if she wasn't touching me, and it seemed this trait had carried over into Winta's rebirth.

Instead of sucking on her clit, as I'd been doing, I switched to twirl my tongue in quick movements that had her breath hitching and her cries growing louder. She was close, and so was I.

I inserted a third finger, firmly pressed my tongue against her clit, and hummed. The brush against her G-spot, in combination with the vibration of my tongue, set her off. She came with a scream, clenching tightly around my fingers. I came with a soft groan as I lapped up every drop she gave me.

Once I finished, I became aware of the silence of the room, the feel of my mates' hunger, and the burn of my mate mark from Visa as my bond with Winta cemented.

I leaned back with a grin, licking my lips and fingers as Winta stared hungrily down at me. I could tell she wanted to return the favor, but this was about her, about reconnecting and rejoicing in the fact that she was alive and once again mine. I couldn't wait to get her naked in my bed though, our skin rubbing together as my other mates pleasured us both while we made love to each other.

"Holy fuck, Dick Slayer," Caspian cursed. "Maybe I should call you the Devourer of Pussies."

The men let out soft, hungry chuckles, but I never pulled my eyes from Winta, who blushed and laughed.

I wasn't about to let Caspian's teasing ruin my mood. My heart felt close to bursting. We weren't going to get many chances to bask in our bonds and to just enjoy being together. If what I'd been through with Visa taught me anything, it was to take any opportunity I could to reinforce the mate bond, and to take every moment I could to show them how much I loved them.

3

THORNE

Shifters didn't typically share their mates. We were a one and done species, so the concept that my mate already had four others, not including Winta, would take some adjusting to. At least... I'd thought it would. That was until I watched my stunningly gorgeous and powerful mate drop to her knees and eat out my best friend. I'd damn near come on the spot. I had wanted to join them more than I'd ever wanted anything.

"I think you need a little bit of meat in the middle of that sandwich." I waggled my eyebrows at Ashera and Winta. The blood flow to my brain was minimal at the moment, so my mouth just didn't stop. "I just happen to be prime, grade A man meat."

Everyone in the room stilled, clearly shocked by my serious come-on skills. All eyes turned toward me, so I grinned and blew the ladies a kiss. I always came up with my best material when I was hard. "I am here for all your man meat needs."

Ashera blinked at me, adorably baffled. Winta, used to my antics by now, groaned loudly as she finished salvaging what she could of her clothes. The succubus had done a number on them, and I was both impressed and jealous. She'd reduced the ceremonial leathers Winta had been wearing to scraps. I wanted my leathers to be scraps.

"Ignore him." Winta shot me a withering look, but it only made my grin spread wider. "He only thinks with his little head."

Winta and I had known each other for a majority of our lives. She'd grown accustomed to my quirks. The others would too, no doubt. We were stuck together for the rest of our lives, after all. My duties required me to be exceptionally serious and always on, so I loved being able to let loose whenever possible, which tended to mean I was a bit over the top.

Ashera snorted back a laugh, which had all of us chuckling in response. She gave me a pat on the chest as she made her way over to one of the desks by the fireplace in the center of the room. This office —our favorite in this palace—functioned as a library and showroom, housing rare tomes and various important artifacts from Qamar's history—items that should have been kept in the former palace, but Vaughn had wanted them removed because he'd rather look at pictures of himself.

The former king had been mildly obsessed with himself, which was putting it lightly. By the time we'd deposed him, he really only cared about his own wealth and status. He'd become completely blind to the plight of the people, and allying himself with Tomas hadn't helped his mental state. If anything, he became paranoid, treating even those he'd once considered close friends as enemies.

"As much as I want to start an orgy right now," Ashera teased, "we need to discuss our next steps. We came here in the hopes of killing Tomas and ended up stepping into a coup."

I released a loud, drawn out grown as a clear illustration of my displeasure over missing an orgy. Who wanted to discuss war strategy when they could be having an orgy? Come on. In case there was any doubt left in my mate's mind as to how I felt about this non-orgy, I also sighed dramatically. My dick needed attention. Now.

Everyone else in this fucking room had already solidified their bond with Ashera. Every other male in this room had been inside my mate's tight pussy while she milked them so hard they exploded inside her.

The thought had me hissing.

Once more, everyone stilled and all eyes turned toward me.

"Someone please tell me I heard what I thought I heard," Caspian whispered. There was a hint of glee in his tone, and my eyes narrowed suspiciously. "Because I'm pretty sure I heard a pussy."

"Oh no," Winta murmured, moving to push Ashera behind the desk before standing protectively in front of her. I didn't miss the look Ashera gave Winta. *Interesting.* My mate was a bit of an alpha herself. Sexy.

"What's the matter?" Caspian taunted. "Is the little kitty going to hiss at me again?"

I turned to focus solely on Caspian, and a low growl built in my chest. The other three males all took a step back, and it appeared the fae was just too stupid to take a hint. I cocked my head to the side, allowing my feline to shine through my eyes. I wanted the arrogant prick to know that a predator was sizing him up, and I wanted him to be well aware that he was my prey. He was about to have a very *bad* day.

It seemed as though brains didn't run in his family, because the fucker just smirked at me and crossed his arms over his chest.

"This is going to be fun." Winta smirked.

It certainly was. *The fucker wants a pussy? I'll show him a fucking pussy.*

I shifted.

My skin stretched taut over my lengthening bones, and fur sprouted out of every pore. I intentionally slowed the shift. I wanted Caspian to be well aware of what was coming for him. My incisors lengthened, jutting past my jaw, and a roar burst from my chest. The sound of snapping bones and tearing skin echoed in the quiet office. No one took their eyes off me.

Finally, after what seemed like ages, I stood before the fae prick in my animal form.

My mate's gasp had my eyes darting over to her. She stared at me with wide eyes, her mouth slightly parted as she took me in—a saber-tooth tiger. We were rare, not quite as rare as dragons, but there weren't many of us left, possibly a few thousand, if that. We were one of the more deadly shifter species—masters of stealth packed with pounds of lethal muscle—which made me perfect to run Qamar's army.

I just couldn't always control my temper.

It was a minor issue, really, and nothing to make a big deal about. It certainly wasn't something that interfered with my daily life at all. But people like this asshole fae who acted as though he owned everything and everyone pissed me the fuck off.

When I was pissed the fuck off, I shifted, and then I made an example out of the sorry excuse of a meat sack who'd pissed me off—usually by eating them.

Rationally, I knew I shouldn't have shifted in the office. My feline was massive, taller than I was in my human form. My coarse fur would be a bitch to get out of the books, and if I wasn't careful, my fangs—now the size of Ashera's entire arm—would easily snap anything or anyone in half. Not surprisingly, I usually broke shit when I shifted inside, but Caspian needed to be taught whom he was dealing with. He needed to understand that with a casual swipe of my massive paw, I'd be able to rip his sorry head from his pitiful body then make a nice little snack out of him.

I growled again, stalking closer to the fae prick, but his smirk just seemed to grow, stoking the flames of my ire.

"You *are* a kitty! Delightful." Caspian shook his head, shooting a smirk toward the still awestruck Ashera. "Dick Slayer, you can't seriously think that this overgrown pet is one of your mates."

Dick Slayer? Was that seriously his nickname for his mate? I snarled and narrowed my eyes, then the rest of what he said sank in. *Pet? Did that prick just call me a fucking pet?*

Without warning, I pounced, ramming into Caspian in the blink of an eye. I knew from training other shifters that being hit with an animal this large, this packed with muscle, was like being hit by a moving mountain. My forepaws slammed against his chest, and he grunted in surprise.

We went down with a crash, our growls ripping through the air as soon as we landed. I could smell his surprise, but he wasn't afraid of me. That could prove to be fatal.

Before I could effectively pin him beneath me, his ice-blue gaze met mine and the tattoos along his face and neck began to glow bright white as he harnessed the weird elemental magic all fae possessed. I snarled and leaned down with an open maw filled with razor-sharp teeth, fully intending to put this fucker into a forced submission hold.

"Aww," Caspian cooed, "the kitty wants to play."

Something tangled around my ankles, jerking me off him. *Fuck.* There was another tug on my ankles as I lunged forward with all of my strength, baring my teeth once again. I sank my incisors into the dark flesh of his neck, and I clamped down, refusing to give up my prey. I'd rip him limb from bloody limb and enjoy every moment of his scream filled torment.

After he was out of the way, I'd cement my bond with Ashera to ensure that none of her other mates attempted to challenge me in such a way again. My ridged cock would guarantee that nothing was left in her delicious pussy so I could fill her with half-demon, half-shifter babies. The thought of a fae free future was vastly appealing to both me and my feline.

"Stop!" My mate's voice cut through the primal haze that had taken over my mind. Whenever I shifted, it was a delicate balance between the rational human side and the primal animal side. Sometimes the animal side started to dominate.

I turned to look at Ashera, my fangs dripping with Caspian's blood. The fae's neck spurted crimson liquid with each thump of his heart. My feline's ears flattened against my skull. Our mate was frowning at us with a glare marring her beautiful features.

"That's enough. Cas, stop with the air magic. Thorne, can you shift back? Please?" The alpha demand in her voice was clear.

To my shock, my feline was more than happy to listen to her. He preened at her attention, pleased that she'd admonished the fae and not me. He deserved to be put in his place, and watching her scold him was hot as fuck. A low, rumbling purr emanated from my chest.

Caspian arched a mocking brow at me, and I was immediately made aware of the phantom-like wisps releasing my ankles. *Air magic*, I scoffed. *Stupid fae.* I was going to have to watch my back around this asshole. There was no telling what sort of shit he'd try to pull when Ashera wasn't looking. What the hell did Ashera see in him anyway?

With one last warning growl, I stepped off and away from Caspian. I moved to one of the corners of the room, well away from anyone so as not to accidentally harm someone when I shifted. I soothed my feline enough to shrink back down into my human form, my bones once again snapping and rearranging themselves. Once I was standing on two legs, I cracked my neck and raised my arms above my head to stretch out the now tight muscles. I was always tight as fuck after a shift.

"You have got to be fucking kidding me!" The outraged yell yanked my focus to another of Ashera's mates, the vampire—Ambrose. He was glaring from me to Ashera and back. He was livid, and his posture screamed hostility. "No. Fuck. No."

I crossed my arms over my chest and snarled at the surly vamp. He seemed a bit dramatic. "What the fuck is your issue, bloodsucker?"

The fae had a death wish, and the vampire was a drama queen, so I had little hope that the angel and the incubus were normal. Although, to be fair, Malachi seemed more on top of shit than anyone else in the group, but with the way these two morons acted, I was starting to question whether Ashera had ever experienced a real man.

I took a moment to study the foursome. Caspian had regained his feet and was no longer bleeding from the neck wound I'd inflicted on him. He was damn lucky I'd only been making a point and hadn't actually gone for the kill. He had this haughty look on his face that had me thinking—despite our height difference—that he was looking down his nose at me. It made me want to punch him in the face. How the fuck did any of Ashera's mates get anything done with this asshole ruining everything he touched? Prick.

Then there was Ambrose. I could have sworn I'd heard someone refer to him as "princess" while they were all at my house. It had been a distant conversation, but thanks to my shifter hearing, I'd been able to make out some of what had been said. The slur suited him if this temper tantrum was anything to go by. Gods, I hadn't seen someone act like this since Winta was a young cub and she'd been denied a dessert because she hadn't finished her dinner. Being that over the top all of the time must be fucking exhausting, not just for Ambrose, but for those around him in particular. I was curious to see if everyone went to bed with a raging headache every night thanks to the annoying prince.

Jacobi, the quiet angel king, seemed far more reserved than the rest. I'd save my judgment of him for later. It was always the quiet ones that you had to look out for. He was a freak in some sense of the word, so I'd keep my eye on him.

Finally, Malachi. He seemed to be the alpha of this merry little band, and I had no real interest in changing that. That being said, he needed to get the morons beneath him to heel before I made them all fucking bleed.

Ashera clearly needed someone to smack a bit more sense into these four. I'd happily slide into the beta position. Bashing in heads was a lot more fun anyway. Although, where that left Winta in the grand scheme of things had yet to be seen. It wasn't rare or odd for females to mate within a harem of mostly males. It wasn't common, but it wasn't unheard of. Just thinking about Winta fitting into Ashera's harem had my mind racing back to my mate pinning the queen against the door and eating her out as though she were trying to lick Winta's soul.

I was still rock fucking hard.

"*That*" —Ambrose pointed to my cock— "is my fucking problem. There is no fucking way—*no fucking way* that is getting anywhere near my mate."

Five sets of eyes swiveled to my proud dick, and I made sure to arch my hips a bit so my mate could get a good eyeful. I also made direct eye contact with Ashera, who licked her lips as heat burned in her green gaze. Most natural felines, those who weren't shifters, had barbed cocks. Shifter felines didn't have barbs, but our cocks were more textured than the average male's. I had small bundles of skin on the shaft of my cock that would swell to hit Ashera's G-spot and any other sensitive area with each movement I made. I'd once heard a female liken it to the piercings some males had that ran down their dicks.

"Ashera," Ambrose growled, "don't tell me that you're going to let that *monster* inside you."

Ashera smirked and looked over at her vampire, who had started to pace between the two of us, his hands flying wildly in the air as he grumbled under his breath. She chuckled softly as she watched him before saying, "He's going to need to play nice before he's allowed entrance. I know that *you* wouldn't know about that, but Cas certainly does."

Jacobi and Malachi both let out dark chuckles. Another inside joke. My feline growled inside my head, and I grumbled my agreement.

Instead of focusing on being left out of the joke, I focused on the first part of her statement. *I'll show you just how good I can be, little mate.* I pumped my fist along my cock a few times before taking a step toward her.

"Little mate, you want to see me play nice?" I purred, taking another step in her direction.

The world tunneled down to just us two. Every time I inhaled, I breathed in her scent, which was still sweet with arousal. Her eyes had dilated with hunger. I wanted to sate that hunger by feeding my cock between those plump lips of hers while I tangled my fingers in her gorgeous golden locks. I wanted to watch Winta slide her fingers into our little mate's sweet pussy as she teased Ashera with her tongue from behind while I fucked that delicious mouth.

Then, I wanted to fuck my little mate raw. I wanted her to scream my name until she couldn't scream anymore. I wanted my come dripping off her. I wanted to mark her in a way that made her other mates know that she belonged to me just as much as she belonged to them. I wanted her so spent that they would have to clean me off of her, and I wanted them to watch every fucking minute.

I took another step closer.

Something primal deep within me was calling out for me to lay claim to her in every way I could imagine. I needed it, needed her, more than I needed my next breath. My ache for her was nearly overwhelming. She was all I could see. All I could smell. All I could hear.

Ashera took a step in my direction, her green eyes heavy with need. She was just as lost to the mating call as I was. I could smell her arousal strengthen in the air around us and could practically taste her sweet pussy on my tongue. My feline was hissing, growling, and clawing beneath my skin, just as desperate as I was to get to our mate. She'd been so focused on giving Winta pleasure, she hadn't completely sated herself. She needed my cock. *Only* my cock.

"No! Absolutely fucking not!" Ambrose's roar slapped me out of my tunnel vision mere inches from my delicious mate. I snarled low in my throat, my fists clenching at my sides as I fought not to break the fucker's face. "There is no way that *thing* is going to fit in you, little queen. I've been in that tight little pussy of yours. He will rip you in half."

What I heard the vamp say was that he was intimidated by my cock. It wouldn't be the first time a male or female had seen my impressive size and felt a bit scared. I tilted my head a bit, my feline surging to the surface to shine out of my eyes. I studied the vamp. Maybe if I fucked *him*, he'd feel more comfortable letting me pin my little mate against any available surface to make her scream. It wouldn't be the first time I'd fucked a male, and I was sure—based on the look of Ashera's harem—it wouldn't be the last.

Just as I was contemplating my method of attack, the angel king snagged my mate around her waist and pulled her away from me, stepping between the two of us. That got my feline's attention. I released a feral snarl and fought the urge to shift again. I hadn't given anyone permission to touch what was *mine*.

"I'm not interested in keeping her from you," Jacobi reassured me as he raised his hands in a placating gesture. "But we aren't here for you to fuck Ashera. We're in your palace to discuss matters of state. When we're all back at your house, perhaps then you can" —he let out a small cough— "figure out your... issue. Waving your cock around is not going to get us through what we need to address any faster, so I suggest you tuck it away for the time being.

As much as I hated to admit it, the feathered cockblock was right. I took several deep lungfuls of air to calm myself. I then nodded and grabbed a blanket from the top of one of the chairs that were scattered throughout the room and wrapped it around my waist. The angel king was far too calm and logical for my liking. Hadn't he felt this overwhelming, overpowering urge to lay claim to Ashera? To mark her? To give her pleasure unlike anything she'd ever known?

At least Ashera looked just as put out by this as I did. It was a small consolation.

No matter, the longer we circled around this, the more explosive we'd be when we finally came together.

~

Ashera

IT TOOK me several moments to calm myself. Heat still surged through my veins, and my succubus cried out for her mate. I knew all too well what waiting to cement the mate bond could do. I wouldn't go back on my word and mate with Thorne until my other mates were ready for me to do so, but I also needed to make sure they knew I couldn't wait forever. Something inside me wouldn't allow that, which meant I needed to have a difficult conversation with Ambrose.

I rubbed my temples as my eyes drifted close at the thought. Having more than one mate was going to drive me insane. Especially *these* mates. The gods were playing some sort of prank on me if they seriously thought giving me six alpha-holes was a good idea. The next one that pissed me off would be sent back to their country in pieces.

"Clearly all the males in the room need a timeout." I glared at all of them when they each released a growl. "Go. Move to a corner. Now. Jacobi, you can stand in the middle of the room. If you're all going to act like children, I'll treat all of you like children."

They grumbled but moved to do as I'd demanded. They glowered at each other, and I had to fight the urge to throttle each one. I wouldn't deny that I was still painfully turned on, but I was more annoyed. They needed to stay away from me, because I wasn't sure if I was going to slap them stupid or fuck each one of them until they didn't know their own damn names.

We didn't have time for petty distractions.

"We need to figure out where to go from here," I said as I gave each one a stern gaze. "We left Masas for the hinterlands before I 'died' and then came straight here because this was where we believed Tomas was. We didn't plan to walk into a coup, and we didn't plan on how exactly we're going to make my death benefit us. We haven't figured *anything* out."

I sighed and massaged my temples again. "We haven't stopped to think. We've been *reacting*, and that needs to stop. All of you should know this is like a game of chess. We need to think at least five moves ahead if we want to come out on top. Right now, we're two steps *behind*. That's unacceptable."

"We're now operating on the assumption that Tomas went to Sahira, to King Judah, but we don't know that for certain," Malachi stated.

I turned to face him. "Do we have any spies in the area who can confirm for us?"

"We do," he replied. "I can get word out that we need a confirmed sighting of King Tomas."

"Former," Ambrose growled.

"You haven't officially deposed him yet," I reminded him. "Which is yet another thing we need to do. How do we want to tackle that?"

I tugged at the ends of my hair, beyond frustrated by the number of things we needed to do. It felt as though we were running out of time, and I didn't want to feel like we had to rush through everything. That was when mistakes happened. Yet I couldn't shake this overwhelming sense of urgency, almost as though if we didn't do everything in the next few moments, the world would come crumbling down around us. The feeling made me itchy.

Winta stepped up beside me and placed her hand on my shoulder, giving it a gentle squeeze. I leaned into the touch, already feeling more at peace. Winta had the same subtle, nurturing aura that Visa had—which wasn't surprising—but with a touch of something... bolder, more laced with steel.

Not all souls, if reborn, came back the same, which made sense. Winta and Visa were two very different people, and it was easy for me to see just how different they were. And yet their soul was still the same bright, warm, and comforting soul it had always been. Words couldn't describe how excited I was to learn more about Winta and our connection. Winta already felt like home.

"Why don't we have Ambrose make an official statement saying that Tomas is no longer fit to rule? He moved in direct opposition, with no provocation, against a ruler of Dunya, and as such, Ambrose has decided to replace him and is now the acting ruler of Masas." Winta was already proving her ability to strategize like a true queen. My pride in her almost burst through my chest. "Malachi can have his spies do some digging, and we can have ours do so as well. We can find out where Tomas really is. In the meantime, we need to gather all loyal troops in every kingdom and prepare for war."

I hated that Winta was right. The knowledge that outright war between the kingdoms was going to be the most likely outcome left an acidic pit in my stomach. Too many innocents would die because of this... because of me. I bit my bottom lip and took a deep breath. More would die if we sat back and did nothing. The death rate for slaves was obscenely high, so we needed to act.

"You're forgetting about Juniya," Caspian added, drawing my attention away from my worries. I groaned. I *had* forgotten about Juniya. "I have no idea how my father will react to all of this. I may need to do something similar to Ambrose. Juniya has stayed out of this, at least I think so, but I can't say that they'll stand aside for much longer, especially not now that Qamar has fallen to a similar coup as Shaytan."

I groaned again. This all felt insurmountable. How the hell could we possibly handle all of this? It felt as though the earth was crumbling beneath my feet and it was only a matter of time before I fell into a large hole that I couldn't find a way out of. *Gods.*

"We should divide and conquer." I regretted the words almost as soon as they came out of my mouth, but I couldn't see any way around it.

All of the males in the room began to argue, and my anger from before started to bubble to the surface again. *They are all getting returned. Morons.* Winta and I locked gazes and rolled our eyes at the bickering. It was really nice to have another female to commiserate with.

I understood why they were opposed to the idea. I did. And I didn't really need my new empathic gifts either. We were all far too raw from my near-death experience. They were also nervous about the changes that were currently raging through my body. None of them wanted to be away in case something happened. I felt the same. My heart was breaking at the thought of sending my mates off to face unknown challenges, of them not being here if my new powers suddenly started to hurt instead of help me. But there was no getting out of this.

We needed to break into groups if we wanted to succeed. I felt it with an odd sense of surety. This was the right course of action.

"Caspian and Jacobi can go to Juniya together. Thorne and Ambrose can head to Masas—" I didn't get to finish before a renewed burst of denial flew from each of them.

"Stop!" I yelled. They all fell silent, stunned by my outburst. "Just stop. Juniya and Malak have been good trade allies for centuries. It makes sense that Jacobi would go with Caspian to show his support and to potentially strong-arm Juniya with the threat of losing the alliance if they don't fall into line.

"And it makes sense that Thorne goes with Ambrose to Masas. Qamar's army is already loyal to Thorne. With his shifter senses, he should also be able to weed out anyone who could be a potential problem. I can't imagine that Masas will have a lot of nobles or soldiers who are eager to join our cause, so you're going to need a strong military presence, even if it's one from another kingdom, to get people to fall in line."

"It will take a long time to get things together in Masas, little queen," Ambrose pointed out.

I knew it could take a while to get things sorted. It wasn't going to be easy, but we couldn't put this off. It was too dangerous. "Right now, we're three kingdoms against three kingdoms. Malak doesn't have the same military presence that Shaytan and Qamar have." My gaze went to my angel. His eyes hardened as he looked at me, determination settling over his features. "Masas and Sahira both have strong militaries, and I'm not sure we could win in a fight against them. Juniya doesn't have the same might as Masas and Sahira, but they have more soldiers than Malak does. Frankly, based on numbers alone, we'd lose without going against Masas and Juniya."

"She's right," Thorne spoke up. "I was able to make sure that the majority of our military was loyal to our cause, as I'm sure you did as well in Shaytan, but Masas and Sahira have a larger population than we do. We've started to up our weapons production, but trade is very important. If we can't secure the materials..."

He didn't need to finish. We all knew what would happen to all the kingdoms if the trade routes fell. That acidic pit in my stomach returned with a vengeance. If I were running the resistance, I'd hit the trade routes, disrupt the flow of commerce and take control of each country one at a time.

Gods.

Large, calloused hands settled on either side of my face, and my gaze locked with Malachi's. I hadn't noticed him move from his corner, but Mal always knew when I needed him. "It's going to be alright, Sher. Let's send Caspian and Jacobi out first, because we're closer to Juniya. They can leave later today, and then we can come up with a more solid plan for Masas. Then, we'll *all* head to Masas, picking up the fae and angel on the way. If we need to deal with Juniya, we can do it then. Once Juniya and Masas have been dealt with, we can decide how we want to deal with Sahira. We should know more about Tomas's location by then."

I could feel their resistance to the plan. I would feel it even without my enhanced abilities. They would rather stay with me than split up. It took a minute for each of them to weigh the options, but they ultimately all agreed.

"We leave small armies in each country to secure borders and ensure that any resistance attacks are quickly dealt with," Mal stated. "We're spread out as we are right now, and that makes things easier for the resistance, especially if they have the support of Juniya, Tomas, and Sahira. They are all connected to the south. If we can even just get Masas under our control, it'll make things a lot easier since it's situated between Sahira and Juniya, making it harder for the two kingdoms to strategize together."

"If I have to leave you assholes alone with her, then I want time with my mate." Caspian pushed Malachi aside and wrapped an arm around me. "The angel can come with us because he's leaving with me, but the rest of you fuckers need to take a hike."

The others grumbled but acquiesced, leaving the three of us alone in the office.

I stepped away from Caspian to rest my hip against the desk, and Jacobi moved to stand beside my fae prince. "Are you both sure you're okay with this plan?"

"I'm not about to lie to you, Dick Slayer. Do I wish we were staying together? Fuck yes. But you and Bat Fuck are right, we can't do it all by staying together in one area, no matter what we want." Caspian ran his hands through his brilliant, white hair. "I don't want to leave you, but I've come to realize that my father could pose a threat to you, and I won't allow that."

Jacobi nodded his agreement. "Caspian is right, my love. We need to ensure your safety. None of us want to see you the way we did mere days ago. If Malak needs to raise an army, we will, and I'll make sure that I help Caspian out in any way possible."

I studied them for a moment, feeling tears sting the backs of my eyes. I honestly didn't want them to separate from the group. After what happened with Visa, finding new mates made me loath to let them out of my sight. But they were all grown men who were older than I was, and warriors too. I had to have faith that they would be able to take care of themselves and each other. Pairing Caspian with Jacobi at least ensured that no one would die on this trip.

"I love you both so much." I stood and made my way between them so they could both wrap their arms around me. "You'd best look out for each other. Caspian, that means not being a dick."

He chuckled against my ear, causing me to shiver. "I suppose for this short duration of time, I can be less of an asshole."

I grinned up at him as Jacobi pressed his lips against the nape of my neck. I released my pheromones, wanting them to lose their tightly held control. They both groaned and pressed against me. I loved the feel of being between two of my mates. They were all so much bigger than I was, harder too.

Jacobi shifted so he could lock eyes with Caspian over my shoulder. "Undress and get on your back, you fae fuck."

Caspian wanted to argue, but he surprised me by giving both of us a wicked grin and doing what he was told... for once. My mouth dropped open as Caspian laid himself on the floor, his eyes glued to me.

"Now you, my love. Strip. Then I want you to sit on the fae fuck's face while you suck his cock." *Gods*. The command in Jacobi's voice did wickedly delicious things to my body.

It was almost embarrassing how quickly my limbs moved to obey him, my mind too hazy with lust to process that I wasn't running the show here. It seemed my angel king had a thing for being in control. I loved it.

Before I knew it, I was straddling Caspian's face and leaning down over his large body to brush my lips against the tip of his cock. Caspian didn't waste any time burying his face in my pussy. He gave me two long licks that had me bucking against him before he focused on my clit.

I moaned as I slipped the head of his dick into my mouth, alternating between sucking and licking the tip. His low growl told me to keep going, so I braced myself on one of his thighs and wrapped my other hand around his base as I continued to tease him.

"I want you to take him deep." Jacobi's deep rumble had me pressing my hips down on Caspian, who wrapped his arms around my hips and pulled me harder against his mouth.

Shifting back, I licked my lips and shuddered at a particularly excellent flick of Caspian's talented tongue. Slowly, I worked my fae's delicious, dark cock into my mouth, not stopping until I had all of him down my throat.

"Good girl, my love."

I preened and swallowed around Caspian, which caused the fae to growl and attack my clit harder.

Suddenly, my hips were lifted and Jacobi's large cock slammed into me. I gasped, releasing Caspian from my mouth. A harsh slap to my ass had my pussy clenching around Jacobi.

"I didn't tell you to stop sucking him." Jacobi spanked me again, and I lowered my head to take Caspian back into my mouth. "Now keep licking that pretty little clit."

Caspian didn't need to be told twice. The two of us worked our strokes in tandem with Jacobi's thrusts, but my sneaky fae wasn't about to be outdone. His tongue started to move from my clit to Jacobi's cock as my angel thrust hard and deep inside me.

"Fuck," Jacobi growled, his thrusts stuttering a bit.

"Your cock tastes amazing covered in Dick Slayer, you feathered douchebag." Caspian tugged my hips harder against his face and kept alternating between licking my clit and licking my angel's dick.

My pussy fluttered, overstimulated by what was happening between my two large mates. I swallowed around Caspian again, causing the fae to curse before sucking on my clit.

My orgasm screamed through me, fast and bright. I hadn't even been aware I was that close to the edge. Both males groaned. Jacobi slammed into me harshly while Caspian sucked on my clit before licking Jacobi's shaft.

"Gods!" Jacobi moaned. "He's got my balls in a fucking vise." Caspian had moved his hand from my hip, and I'd been wondering where it went.

I sucked on Caspian harder, moving my own hand to massage the fae's balls. He bucked under me, then I hummed around him, and he cursed loudly.

"Make her come again, you feathered fuck. I'm about to burst down her throat." Caspian turned his attention back to my clit, sucking it into his mouth.

Jacobi leaned back, thrusting rough and fast. I loved every second of his pounding pace. He slipped a finger into my ass at the same time Caspian sucked on my clit. Gods, I was so close. My pussy clamped down around Jacobi's cock.

"Suck my balls, you annoying dick," Jacobi demanded. Caspian's lips left my clit, and it was enough to set me off.

I came with a scream around Caspian, who came with me, emptying down my throat. Moments later, Jacobi came with a roar, his hips slapping against mine a few more times.

"You didn't feed, my love," Jacobi murmured as he pulled out of me.

"Yeah, Dick Slayer. You should have fed." Caspian ran his tongue along my slit and hummed at the taste of Jacobi and me. "You need to make sure you're staying strong for whatever other changes your body decides to throw at you."

"I'm okay," I assured them, moving off Caspian to sit on the floor. Jacobi handed me his shirt to clean myself with. "I'll make sure I stay well fed."

I leaned over to plant my lips on Caspian's. He framed my face with his hands as he deepened the kiss. It was soft and tender, the complete opposite of my fae mate. I was once again fighting back tears when I pulled away.

"If either of you die, I'm going to bring you back and kill you myself." I glared at them. Jacobi chuckled before lowering his head to kiss me.

"I promise, my love, we'll be safe." I wished I could believe it would be that easy.

4

WINTA

"General Thor—I mean... Your Majesty?" One of our warriors— Bradford—ran into the kitchen of Thorne's home where Thorne, Ashera, her two remaining mates, and I had been having breakfast. Bradford was just as tall as Thorne and had dark skin like me, but he had shockingly blond hair that he wore long and tied at the nape of his neck. He also had bright green eyes and a closely shaved beard. He was relatively handsome as far as shifters went. Thankfully, the young shifter was utterly loyal to Thorne and could be trusted with knowing that Ashera was alive. Only two other guards in Qamar knew that she was here. That decision had been made yesterday strictly out of necessity. If we were down two of Ashera's mates, we needed additional eyes on our beloved mate.

After saying goodbye to Caspian and Jacobi, they'd headed to Juniya to talk with Caspian's father. We'd finalized more of our strategy and finally headed back to Thorne's home to crash. Since Thorne's home was closer to the center of the capital, it was better for us to stay here and commute to the summer palace for the time being until we could build a new palace over the ashes of the old one. We wanted to be close to the true seat of power in Qamar. The summer palace was just for formality anyway. Thorne's estate was large enough that we would be able to see any nobles or soldiers we needed to.

I'd spent the night wrapped around my mate. Her warm, golden skin had instantly lulled me to sleep. In truth, I had never felt the intense ecstasy I'd experienced when Ashera knelt before me. The logical part of me knew that was because I had never been with my mate before, but a small part of me couldn't help but wonder if that was Visa coming through. Our time together yesterday, although brief, had shown me exactly what having Ashera as a mate was going to be like. I needed to find a moment to show her just as much pleasure as she'd shown me.

My mind circled back to Visa. I knew Ashera respected me for who I was, but how could I ever hope to replace Visa, a lost mate? The two of them had been together longer than I had been alive. I shook my head, forcing myself to compartmentalize those thoughts like a good little soldier. We had enough problems in front of us without me being concerned about being my mate's original mate reincarnated. That was just a mind fuck.

Thorne, of course, had been extremely irritated that he hadn't been allowed into the bedroom. I had no doubt he'd find his place with the other males in Ashera's harem, he just needed to earn it first. Thorne was still trying, comically, to get into Ashera's leathers every second he could manage. Ambrose would only let that happen over his cold, lifeless corpse. Even now, Thorne was sliding his hand toward Ashera's leg, the curve of her thigh tightly wrapped in her fighting leathers. The vampire's entire body was clenched as though he was about to leap across the table and strangle Thorne. Leave it to a man to fight something that anyone in their right mind could see was completely inevitable. I'd known him for decades, and I'd never known him to fail at getting what he wanted.

Thorne wanted his mate.

I couldn't blame Thorne for his tenacity. Even I wanted to run my tongue across her smooth golden skin, drag my nails down her back, and hear her moan my name. She was extremely hard to resist. This would all eventually come to a head, and I was eagerly awaiting the fallout since the two of them were both dramatic as fuck.

Bradford's nervous cough as he anxiously shifted from foot to foot drew me out of my musings. I smiled at him, willing to take pity on him since it appeared as though Thorne had no real interest in paying attention to the poor male, choosing to provoke Ambrose instead.

"Bradford, there's no need to address Thorne that way. He may have the title on paper, but he has yet to prove he's earned it." Thorne choked on the next bite of his breakfast, shooting me a glare. I simply gave him a smug smile. "What is it?"

Bradford's gaze bounced between Thorne and me before settling squarely on me. He seemed less nervous, which was good.

"Queen—" He stuttered, but I waved off the title. "Your Majesty, I just received a report that a small army has been spotted heading toward the gates. They should arrive within the hour."

We all froze. A small army? This was a direct act of war on Qamar. Who the hell would be so foolish? Thorne, whose attention was now wholly focused on the young soldier, leaned forward. "Roughly how many? We need to determine whether this is a scouting party or an actual declaration of war."

"Regardless," I snapped, "even sending a large contingent of scouts is an act of aggression."

"I agree," Thorne replied. "I doubt it's from Juniya. Caspian and Jacobi wouldn't have made it that far yet. It's possible they made a detour to Malak and sent some of their army—"

"The flags were from Sahira," Bradford interrupted.

"That fucker," Ambrose muttered under his breath. "We should have known that snake, King Judah, would pull something like this."

My mind ran several miles a minute as I attempted to anticipate all the possibilities ahead of us. It was possible Judah had come to simply check on things in Qamar. There had been a few individuals who fled after we'd beheaded my father. It was entirely possible that Judah brought a small contingent with him to check on the status of the country. Unrest in one kingdom could quickly spiral into unrest in other kingdoms, as Ashera's coup had already proven.

My history with Judah—an arranged engagement that was never going to amount to anything—was murky at best. I'd thought we were friends when I was younger, but roughly seventy-five years ago, Judah had suddenly become distant and moody. I wanted to believe that he hadn't come here to harm my people, but we hadn't had any sort of consistent contact with one another since he'd changed and become a bit reclusive.

Thorne stood with his hands on the table, forcing me back to the matter at hand. "Are the gates closed?" I asked him.

He nodded. "They've been closed and closely guarded since we discovered this lot." He gestured at our mate and her males.

That would give us time to come up with a quick plan and make it out to meet Judah. It wasn't much, but I'd take it. The others got to their feet, and the screech of chairs scraping along the tiles had Thorne and I cringing.

Malachi, who always seemed to be prepared, was tightening the straps that held his blades against his leathers, while Ambrose had a murderous gleam in his eyes. I had a feeling I would need to remind both of them that we wanted to avoid killing Judah—at least for now.

Ashera started making her way to the door. I admired the fact that she didn't even flinch in the face of a conflict, but...

"You can't go out there like that, Ashera." My words stilled her, and she whirled to glare at me.

Her expression became mutinous, and it turned me on almost as much as it worried me. She huffed and crossed her arms before she said, "Why not? This is our chance to sway Sahira to our side. Or at the very least get some answers."

I shook my head, stepping over to her so I could rub her arms in an attempt to soothe her ire. "The kingdoms still believe you're dead, Ashera. You made the decision to be a ghost, and it's important that you continue to do so. We're too deep to have you reveal yourself now. All we need is one person to mention they saw a demon that looked like Shaytan's queen, and we'll be flooded with resistance members."

"I can't sit here while you and the others face an army, Winta. You're my mates! I won't let you face that alone." Her eyes hardened as she clasped my hands.

"I'm not saying that you need to let us do this alone." I softened my voice. "I'm asking you to do this wisely. We need to play the long game if we want to win."

Ashera groaned softly and closed her eyes. That was when I knew I had her.

"You're right," she grumbled. "I hate that you're right, but you are."

"I know," I replied gently. "Why don't we get you in your cloak and then you can come with us? There are two watchtowers on either side of the gate. You can head up one of those and have a bird's eye view of everything that happens. The space is pretty open too, so you should be able to hear everything unless we're whispering."

She huffed, but her shoulders relaxed, indicating that I'd made my point. I knew this was hard for her. Hell, it was hard for all of us, but we'd committed to this course and needed to see it through. I leaned in to kiss her cheek and she relaxed a little more.

"You'll be part of this, Ashera. I promise."

"Thank you, Winta." She brushed her lips against mine.

Running on pure impulse, I leaned into the kiss, deepening it. I slid my tongue along the seam of her lips until she opened for me, and our tongues started to dance. My world boiled down to this moment. Her. In my arms. I hated that I couldn't take any more than just this brief meeting of mouths.

We pulled away all too soon. Surprisingly, the men in the room weren't rushing us, and it appeared they were giving us privacy. I narrowed my eyes at them suspiciously, but they weren't acting overly innocent, so I didn't make a fuss.

"I'll show my little mate to the towers by the gates," Thorne offered as he stepped over to us.

Ambrose turned an alarming—and if I was being honest, extremely amusing—shade of purple. His chest, which was constantly bared to show off his exceptionally large mate mark, was puffed out, and if looks could kill, Thorne would already be very, *very* dead.

"Like fucking hell you are!" the vamp roared as he wedged himself between Thorne and Ashera. "You're going to keep that mutant cock away from my mate."

Thorne's eyes narrowed, but a sharp look from both Ashera and me stopped him before he made any attempt to dismember the arrogant asshole. The two of them were certainly going to have to work on that.

"Bradford is mated," I pointed out.

Before I could even open my mouth to continue, Ambrose grunted and stated, "He's the one who will take Ashera to the tower." He spun to glare at the soldier. "I'm only trusting you because you're mated. If you try anything, I'll know. You don't want to know what I'll do to you, understand? And *you!*" He spun to stab a finger in Thorne's direction. "You and that abomination you call a cock will stay away from Ashera. No man meat, no hidey-holes, no *nothing.*"

Bradford looked over to Thorne for help, but he was too busy attempting to murder the vampire prince with his glare. The young male gulped, nodded, and bowed his head.

Ambrose draped Ashera's cape over her before leading her over to Bradford, making sure to keep his body between Ashera and Thorne. My gaze drifted to Mal, and I raised a brow.

"Unfortunately, he's always like this. We're trying to house train him, but he's also an idiot, so it's taking time." The deadpan tone he used while delivering that information had me chuckling as I moved out of the kitchen and down the hall, the others following closely behind me.

Thankfully, we were mostly prepared to leave. We gathered our weapons, which Thorne made us keep by the door because he was a neat freak and had a place for everything. Gods help whoever left anything out where it wasn't supposed to be.

∽

Ambrose

I KNEW I was being unreasonable. I knew Ashera and Thorne were meant to be mates and would eventually finalize the bond.

But I was still feeling raw about the disaster with my father.

Malachi had actually pulled me aside again yesterday to tell me that a little introspection wouldn't be a bad thing in this situation. I supposed he could be right... possibly. He probably wasn't, but I'd think on my actions for my little queen. After all, I wasn't the one with the cock built for killing people. *Fucking cat.*

Was I really being unreasonable if the godsdamned cat had a death cock? I shook my head. No. I wasn't being unreasonable. I was protecting my mate from certain death. Impaling people on pikes wasn't exactly a pleasant death. My little queen had taught me that needlessly killing people was wrong, so I wasn't about to unnecessarily send her to her death over some fucking feline.

No.

Thorne was the unreasonable one in this situation. He expected *my* little queen to hop on his cock and not instantly be split in two. How fucking selfish was that?

It took me a moment to realize that the others were well ahead of me, my little queen following the young soldier from the kitchen. At least she was away from the fucking cat. The urge to remind my little queen that I could give her anything that fucking useless feline could and more hit me hard, so I slipped away from the others as they headed directly for the gates.

～

Ashera

I WAS STILL irritated by the idea of remaining in the shadows while my mates faced an unknown threat. We knew King Judah was coming with a small contingent of men, but we really had no idea why he'd come and just how well trained those men were. For all we knew, they were meant to be a distraction from an attack elsewhere in the kingdom. I felt jittery at just the thought.

I trailed behind Bradford. He kept casting nervous glances my way as though he expected me to knock him out and do something foolish. Which, if I was being completely honest with myself, wouldn't be out of the realm of possibility if I wasn't attempting to keep a low profile. I'd appreciated Winta's reminder, even if it had stung. This was my idea, and it was a damn good one. I shouldn't throw it away. I should trust that my mates could handle this. I did. I just didn't want them to do it alone... not that they were actually alone. Gods! I was such a torn up mess.

I took a deep breath and let it out slowly, centering myself. Getting anxious was the easiest way to fuck things up.

The walk from Thorne's house to the capital's gates didn't take long. He wasn't quite on the outskirts of the city, but he was close enough that the jaunt was pleasant. We strolled down the main street of Zvezda. It was lined with stalls selling fresh produce, meats, jewelry, cloth, and all manner of other things. People were happily chatting as they shopped, and children ran wild in the streets, laughing and playing. It was clear that even though Winta and Thorne had upended the status quo, the people weren't threatened by the change. It spoke volumes about their people's trust in them. Pride burst through me as my gaze found my two newest mates. They already had their people's love and trust.

I adjusted my hood over my face to ensure that no one could see me. I couldn't hear the hoofbeats of the witches' horses yet, so they weren't too close. That settled my nerves even more. My mates had time to plan, and I had time to get into position to ensure that nothing went wrong.

The gates, made of wrought iron with sharp pointed tips, soared toward the sky. The metal at the heart of the gates was molded into breathtakingly detailed dragons. I was extremely impressed with the craftsmanship. Despite being ornate, it appeared sturdy and able to keep out anything unwanted from the city's center. The two towers on either side were taller than the gates, almost as tall as the old trees that lined the walls on the city's side. They were made of stone and looked weathered with age, though not shabby. It was going to be a long climb to the top. The thought had me grimacing.

As I started to climb the winding stairs, I realized just how fucked we could all be. I hadn't intended to start a war throughout Dunya when I'd sought to overthrow Shaytan's former king. I had only wanted vengeance for my mate and freedom for my people. Gods, I'd been naïve to think that my rebellion wouldn't impact the other kingdoms so deeply. Wasn't that what I'd wanted? Hadn't I hoped the other kingdoms would rebel and become like Shaytan?

I'd even determined that if they didn't instigate change in their own kingdoms that I would assist, but I didn't realize exactly what that meant until now. How many lives would be lost? I'd been stupid enough to believe that we could happily skip from one kingdom to another until they were all free. I hadn't actually stopped to consider that they wouldn't just be fighting inside their own borders, but that they would be fighting each other too.

I rubbed my temples. Gods. I certainly hadn't expected it to all come to a head all at once like this. Though I absolutely should have realized this was the most likely outcome.

I hadn't intended to start this war, but there was no way I wouldn't end it.

War, dark and bloody, was on the horizon for Dunya, and no matter what we did now, we wouldn't be able to stop it. It would come to gory battlefields and legions, death and destruction. If I was going to end this war, I would do it in a manner that ensured my mates were left standing at the end, no matter the cost I had to pay to the gods. When I'd fought against Shaytan's armies, those who remained loyal to the king, they'd face a young succubus who had just lost her mate.

The armies I'd face now were in for a nightmare. I might not fully understand my new powers, but I'd use them without question to see victory.

"Y-Your Highness?" Bradford whispered. I'd completely forgotten he had led me up the stairs to a small room that had windows facing in every direction.

"Don't use my title," I admonished. "It's not safe."

"I apologize. I tried getting your attention, but you were lost in thought. But... your, uh—" He gestured out the side window.

The leaves in the trees nearest that window were swaying almost violently. I'd accidentally released my elemental abilities while thinking about the coming war. I took a deep breath and centered myself again, calming my mind and raging emotions. The wind died down instantly. I never had a problem controlling the elements before, but I was changing now. I had no idea what I was fully capable of anymore. I'd need to start meditating regularly again if this kept happening.

Bradford relaxed, a small smile creasing his face. "You can see everything from here. I'm going to go down and join the rest. I made sure no one saw us enter. You'll be safe."

"Thank you," I murmured.

After Bradford left, I moved to the window that faced the gates, clearly able to see my mates gathered with their warriors below as well as out into the distance. There was still no sight of the witches, but I could feel the magic in the air. They were closing in. The small hairs on my arms and neck rose as the anticipation mounted.

My gaze traveled back to my mates. It was hard not to watch them as danger danced in the atmosphere. Three of them—where the hell was Ambrose?—stood in front of the gates, talking with their heads close. A small battalion of shifters were at their backs, ready to fight if the need arose. The males were all shirtless, and the females wore what resembled loin cloths. I supposed it made sense. There was no use shredding quality clothes if you needed to shift in an instant.

I continued to search for Ambrose. *Where is that fucker?*

A hand covered my mouth before I could even sense that someone was in the room with me. I took a deep breath at the same moment my assailant spoke.

"Little queen, you should know better than to leave your back exposed," Ambrose whispered against my ear, sending a shiver of lust down my spine.

I pushed away from him, and he released me so I could turn and look him in the eye. I glared when I saw the mirth in his gaze. "You're an asshole. Why the hell are you up here? You're supposed to be down there with them." I pointed toward the rest of my mates, who were preparing for the approaching army.

"They don't need me." He shrugged. "You and I have unfinished business. Besides, the last time I left you alone, you were kidnapped. That isn't happening again."

My hands made their way to his chest. "What do you mean by unfinished business?"

He lowered one hand to my hip and pushed the hood of my cloak back with his free hand so he could tangle his fingers in my hair. Ambrose's ruby red gaze seemed to glow in the dim light of the room as he pulled me closer. "Don't play coy, little queen."

I huffed. "I'm not. What the hell are you talking about?"

"You were going to let that shifter fuck you in front of me," he snarled.

I rolled my eyes and returned my attention to the window. "He's my mate, Ambrose. You're going to have to accept that. We don't have time for your petty shit right now. An army is heading right for us."

Ambrose plastered himself against me, using the hand in my hair to turn my face toward his. His thick erection ground against my stomach, causing me to shiver again. He moved his hand from my hair to wrap his fingers around my throat, squeezing just enough to ensure he had my full attention. "The witch army isn't going to be here for a while yet." Another small squeeze. "He may be your mate, and I may need to accept it at some point, but not before you know that you belonged to me well before that asshole ever entered the picture."

The hand he had anchored to my hip moved to unclasp my cloak, the material landing in a puddle at my feet with a soft swoosh. My heart softened a bit. I hadn't realized how vulnerable Ambrose was feeling, and he'd just laid himself bare before me, so I wouldn't give him a hard time about this. It was clear he needed it.

"If the army isn't going to be here for a while" —I leaned in to whisper against his lips— "what do you have planned?"

"I'm going to show you who is in charge here, little queen." I arched an eyebrow at that. How cocky of my vampire. But I was interested in seeing how this would play out, so I didn't respond, letting him take the reins.

His grip around my throat eased, and both of his hands came to rest against the neckline of my training leathers. With a quick tug of his hands, the fabric ripped cleanly down the middle. My nipples tightened against the cool breeze, but it was the hungry, predatory look in Ambrose's eyes that had my back arching in invitation.

"Fuck, little queen," Ambrose growled.

My vampire surprised me. Instead of attacking my skin with his mouth, he tackled me to the ground, pressing his legs against my arms to keep me still. He'd moved so fast, I hadn't seen him remove his pants in the process. I'd been severely underestimating my vamp mate if he could move that quickly. Not only had he snuck up on me, but now he'd removed his pants and pinned me to the ground in a single move. It was impressive and hot as fuck.

The glint of metal drew me out of my musings, and I tracked the movement of a blade as it flashed before my face. My gaze flew back to Ambrose as I licked my lips. What was my princess planning?

"I'm going to get you all bloody, little queen. I'm going to use our blood to paint you like a canvas while I fuck these perfect tits of yours." His tone had taken on a husky rumble that sent sparks straight to my core. "I'm going to embed myself so deeply inside you that no one would ever mistake my claim."

I sank my teeth into my lower lip as I nodded. I wasn't sure I could form a coherent response even if I wanted to.

The blade flashed as Ambrose sliced into my skin, but I didn't feel the pricks because after each strike, my vampire leaned down to swipe his tongue seductively along the wound. It made me a panting, needy mess. It also aroused my bloodlust. My desire to sink my fangs into my mate's flesh was almost painful in its intensity.

Ambrose leaned up, slicing his palm as he did so. He dribbled blood in the valley between my breasts before running his palms along both nipples, pinching them so my back arched off the stone floor. He chuckled, a dark rumbling sound that had me moaning.

I'd never thought I could be so aroused by blood, and yet, with Ambrose, it just made sense. He called to something dark inside me, something that found sexual pleasure in the spilling of this life-giving liquid. It was made even more potent knowing I couldn't move to touch or taste him.

"Lift your head and open your mouth, little queen. You're going to suck the head of my cock while I fuck these tits." He gripped his throbbing cock and stroked. Once. Twice. "If you don't do as I say, I won't let you feed off me."

I bit the inside of my lip, wanting to issue a sharp retort, but I'd said I wanted to see this through and let Ambrose take the lead. So I nodded and raised my head, ready to suck his cock with each thrust he made between my breasts.

After adjusting his stance above me, Ambrose lowered his hips to swirl his cock in our mixed blood. We both moaned. He pressed my breasts together, pinching my nipples with his forefingers and thumbs as he did. Our gazes locked, and I could see his insecurities playing out in front of me.

"I'm yours," I murmured softly.

With a loud groan, Ambrose thrust his cock between my breasts, and I swiped the tip of my tongue along its head as he paused with a look of heated bliss on his face. I loved this vampire more than words could ever possibly express.

"I love you," I said as he pulled back.

"Say it again," he demanded as he started to set a relentless pace.

"I love you," I sang between swipes of my tongue against the head of his cock.

He continued to pinch and twist my nipples as he pistoned against my chest. A grunted curse was the only warning I had before he came all over my breasts, his eyes locked on mine.

"You're not going to come until later, little queen. You need to think about everything we've talked about."

I narrowed my eyes on him. I'd let it slide for now, after all, there was an army marching our way, but I was most certainly going to get him back for this. Ambrose pulled away from me. "I'm going to leave you like this, little queen. Covered in my blood and come. You aren't allowed to clean yourself off until that fucking feline has had a chance to smell you."

I sighed. "You're so dramatic."

He opened his mouth to respond, but a shout from outside had us both scrambling to our feet to gaze out the window.

"Get down there now."

"Ashera—"

"*Now!*"

5

MALACHI

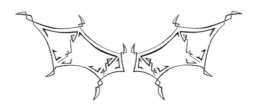

We really didn't have the fucking time for Ambrose's issue with Thorne. The Qamar leader seemed decent... for a shifter. They tended to be full of themselves and arrogant pricks, but after meeting Caspian, they all seemed perfectly normal now. I'd yet to meet anyone who could top the fae prince's ego. Thorne didn't even come close, so that couldn't be Ambrose's main issue with the feline. Regardless of what the problem really was, he was going to need to get over himself. There was no way I was going to allow Ashera to suffer from an incomplete mate bond again.

Thinking about my perfect little slut had my cock stiffening uncomfortably in my pants. I needed to focus, but there was nothing better than watching Sher fall apart with one or more cocks buried deep inside her. I wasn't picky when it came to pleasuring my queen. So long as we were both well fed, and the other assholes in our small group respected Sher, I had no issue with them.

If Ambrose was truly upset by the size of the shifter's cock, it showed just how immature the vampire was. It wasn't about the size, it was how you used it and everything else in your skill set that mattered. Perhaps I'd need to have another chat with the fanged fucker. I rolled my eyes and a grin spread across my lips at the thought. If I did it in front of Ashera, she might just get off on watching me beat the shit out of him.

My gaze landed on Winta, who cocked her head at my smile. I shook my head. There was no need to get into it now. Not that I would need to explain that anything that had to do with Ashera made me grin like a fool. She knew that all too well by now.

Now that there was another female in Ashera's harem, I was interested to see how the dynamics would play out. We'd happily fuck each other for her pleasure, but would that now include Winta? She was an attractive female, but—like with the men—I didn't feel a pull toward her. We'd have to all sit down and discuss how this was going to happen.

I pulled myself out of my thoughts to focus on the road that led to the gates. I could see a dust cloud rising in the distance. The witches would be here soon. I glanced around at our small contingent of soldiers. I hoped like hell we were going to be able to talk some sense into Judah before things got bloody. I was happy to let Winta take the lead in this, as Qamar was her kingdom, but as acting King of Shaytan, I would need to ensure that our interests were clearly represented as well.

I needed to redden Ashera's pert little ass over that stunt. Making us all kings... What the fuck was she thinking?

If they were here to argue about freed slaves, we had plenty of talking points to warm Judah up to the idea of peacefully releasing Sahira's slaves. Shaytan had proven that it was possible to go from a kingdom that survived off the slave trade to a kingdom without slaves. Malak had never had slaves in their entire history, so it was certainly possible. We didn't need to make money off those weaker than us. I was well aware that old habits died hard, and Sahira thrived off the slaves' souls for their magic. It wouldn't be an easy fight to get them to our side.

I fucking hated witches.

I turned to say something to Ambrose, only to find the fanged fucker missing. *Where the fuck is he?*

A moment later, I felt Ashera's arousal and bloodlust spike through the bond. I pinched the bridge of my nose, even as my cock sprang to attention. I noticed Winta shifting uncomfortably as the sensations traveled to her as well. While I wasn't one to deny my mate a solid feeding, especially with her ever changing powers, now was really not the time.

It was just another reason to beat the asshole senseless later.

I'd need to get payback on the bloodsucker for this. I smirked. Jacobi, for all his innocence, would be more than happy to help in that endeavor. Perhaps we could fuck the attitude out of the uptight fae prince while we were at it.

I shook my head, determined to ignore the flood of emotions coming through the bond, and returned my focus to the army that was now within view and galloping straight for us. Based on the number of soldiers, this appeared to be a show of force rather than an actual attack. Perhaps they had come here planning on pressuring the people of Qamar to revolt against their new rulers. Hell, it was entirely possible they'd come all this way based on something Vaughn had done before he lost his head.

I moved to stand behind Winta as a clear display of allegiance. I crossed my arms over my chest, and I made sure I had my best scowl in place as the first riders halted in front of the gates.

"I'd like to talk to Judah first. If we can avoid an attack, that would be the best option for both sides. Let's try to keep things as peaceful as possible," Winta commanded softly. "As much as I'd like to wipe the floor with these assholes, showing our hand too soon, especially while Juniya and Masas are still up in the air, could make things a lot worse for us in the long run."

Thorne just grunted, clearly not liking the idea of playing nice. I couldn't blame him, they'd just tried to kill our mate. I wasn't exactly in the mood to make new friends myself.

"King Judah!" Winta called as the Sahirian king stopped in front of his troops. "I wouldn't have expected you to lead an army to Qamar like this."

Judah dismounted without a word and stood before his army with his arms crossed over his large chest. He was roughly the same height as Jacobi, but he was far more slender than any of the males I'd come to call family. That didn't mean he looked weak—far from it. While I was all bulk, Judah was lean muscle. He carried himself in a way that suggested he was well trained and far stronger than he appeared.

He had shaggy black hair that fell to his chin and piercing, almost neon blue eyes. His skin was almost as pale as Ambrose's, suggesting the witch king didn't get out of the palace much. Something about him —I couldn't quite tell what—felt off. I'd bet anything he was hiding something. I'd even put money on it.

"I wasn't expecting Qamar to fall to rebels." Judah's voice was surprisingly deep. "And yet, here I stand, in front of King Vaughn's daughter—both usurper and executioner." His eyes slid to Thorne. "And her pet cat."

I found myself growling along with Thorne. We, Ambrose in particular, might be making the shifter king work for his place within our group, but that didn't mean anyone else got to put him down. Winta merely canted her head and narrowed her eyes.

"Now, Judah," Winta admonished, dropping his title in a deliberate slight, "is that any way to treat an old ally? My father wasn't fit to rule, so I removed the problem. As his sole heir, it was only natural that I assume the throne upon his death."

Judah snarled, and a taste of the strength that lay beneath the surface bubbled through. "It wasn't your place to question your king."

"I just think you're ass hurt you won't be able to marry Winta and gain a second kingdom now," Thorne taunted. *Interesting*. I hadn't known there was an arranged marriage between the two of them.

I chuckled softly to myself as the lanky man before us turned purple with his rage. I must have been louder than I thought, because his gaze moved to me. I knew the instant he realized who I was. His pupils dilated, and he sucked in an enraged gasp.

"You are harboring this scum?" He flung his finger in my direction. "I can see where your idea of a coup came from."

The witch king moved toward me. I raised a brow in response, flaring my wings slightly to make me look like a bigger threat. Judah flinched ever so slightly, but I knew I had him. Coward.

The air around Winta seemed to still before becoming blazing hot, and sweat began to roll down my back. I knew that this was just a hint of her dragon rearing its head. Pride unexpectedly burst through me.

She was just like Ashera, and she wasn't about to take shit from any man.

"This scum, as you put it, is the King of Shaytan and should be addressed with respect." The bite in Winta's tone couldn't be ignored, and I knew that Ashera would be bursting with love and pride for her mate. "How either of us came into power doesn't matter. What matters is that the former rulers of our kingdoms are dead, and we have filled the vacancy left in their wake. Take it or leave it."

Bravo. I was pretty sure if I started applauding right now, Judah would attempt to kill us all, so I remained motionless. Smug satisfaction oozed throughout my body. She was a very worthy mate for Ashera, and a worthy recipient of Visa's fighting spirit.

I knew little of the King of Sahira, but I didn't recall him being this much of a dick. I searched my memories for small bits of information on King Judah from when I'd been an assassin, but nothing overly important stuck out. Shaytan never had much of an issue with the witch king. From what I could remember, he was a bit of a recluse, keeping to himself and using his envoys to carry out most of his day-to-day tasks. Honestly, Ashera would have known more, and I would need to ask her the next time we all sat down.

It was clear, however, that things had changed. The man that stood before me now was no recluse. He carried himself with a confidence that suggested this man never hid. My senses were screaming at me that something wasn't right, but I still couldn't determine what was actually amiss. Regardless of how this played out, I was going to make sure we kept a very close eye on Judah.

∼

Winta

I STUDIED Sahira's king with narrowed eyes, trying to find any hint of the young man I'd known when I was a child. I hadn't thought it was possible for a person to change so much, even with years of distance between us. It felt as though I was looking at a total stranger. Even his scent was slightly different than it had been. I couldn't explain it. It troubled me... and it had my heart aching at the loss of a good, dependable friend.

Judah had always been aloof. The witches were a standoffish community as a whole, and Judah, being raised as the crown prince, was no different. But he had never been a jerk, which was exactly how he was acting right now. This attitude wasn't like the young prince I'd known at all.

Neither one of us had really wanted to marry the other, but considering both of our fathers were set on the match, we attempted to at least be friendly toward each other. I'd learned that he had a younger twin brother who was never around—always off training for the army, since the king had no need for a spare heir—and that their mother had died giving birth to them, not that his father had seemed to care all that much.

Judah was only about fifteen years older than I was and had been a quiet young man when I'd known him. He'd been kind enough to help me learn about how witches' magic worked and about the history of Dunya and its kingdoms. The man standing in front of me now seemed more inclined to kick a puppy than help a young princess find her way in the world.

If we hadn't been friendly, and our kingdoms hadn't been such close allies, I would have smote him where he stood. My dragon certainly wanted me to roast him. Obviously, he'd spent too much time locked up in his castle to realize that the real world didn't kiss his ass. I'd clearly avoided a mistake when I'd killed my father and mated with Ashera.

I struggled to understand what had happened and how he could change so drastically in such little time. The Judah in front of me was filled with anger and vitriol. He was still glaring at me as though I was a bug he wanted to squish under his boot.

My dragon reared up again, ready to put this witch and all those who followed him in their place. How dare he come to my home, my kingdom, and treat me and my guests like this? I refused to be disrespected in such a manner. I refused to allow men like Judah, like my father, to step all over me ever again. Fury bubbled unchecked through my veins. I'd wipe the earth of—

A gentle touch on my arm surprised me. Malachi gripped my bicep lightly and shook his head slightly. The touch and the head shake were enough to help me rein in my anger. The incubus was right. This wasn't the time nor the place. I needed to focus on attempting to sway Judah to our side. That wouldn't happen if I lost my temper and killed him. I nodded in thanks before turning back to the witch king.

"Really?" Judah smirked condescendingly. "You're going to let the demon scum dictate what you do? Doesn't sound all that different from your daddy's reign. Unless maybe you're sucking the horned bastard's cock."

Before I had a moment to think, let alone respond, a blur of fur and claws shot past me. *Fuck.* Shifters were a temperamental bunch, it came with the dual nature of our souls. I should have known that Thorne was eager to shed Judah's blood, that he'd react instead of speak.

Fuck!

Judah's face contorted into a mess of anger and fear as Thorne wriggled his way through the bars of the gates. *Fuck!*

"Open the gates!" I shouted. There was no way I would leave Thorne to face Judah and his witches alone.

The gates swung open silently as Thorne tore into the short distance between us and the witches.

"Don't just stand there! Attack! Attack for the gods' sakes! Protect your king!" Judah screamed.

Pathetic coward. He wouldn't even fight back? He'd send his men to fight against a single shifter?

I took a deep inhale before raising my arm, my hand fisted. Exhaling, I swung my arm down. The shifters behind me charged, shifting into their animal forms as they rushed past me.

Shouts rang out as both sides attacked without mercy. The metallic tang of blood spoiled the calming natural scents of the trees around us, and the soft ripping of seams rent the air as muscles and bones realigned to form new, more powerful bodies. It was sheer chaos.

Thorne was toying with Judah, who had climbed onto his mount in an effort to avoid the large shifter. For some reason, he wasn't using any of his magic... yet. He'd been quick to scream for his people to attack, and yet he wasn't even trying to defend himself. My eyes narrowed as I studied him. *What is he up to?*

My dragon roared to be free and rain fire down on those who dared to challenge us, but I held her back. I wanted to observe Judah and his witches. Something felt off, and I wasn't about to engage until I was certain this wasn't a trap.

Malachi was working his way toward Thorne and Judah, efficiently taking out any witch that got in his way. For a man used to killing in the shadows, he knew how to move on a battlefield. His former king had been stupid to only use his assassin skills.

"Get back, you beast!" Judah's shout had me once again focusing on him and Thorne. "If you fucking touch me, I'll take out your precious queen with a thought!"

I snorted a laugh. Thorne was making Judah's horse prance with nerves as he circled the pair. I rolled my eyes. He needed to stop toying with them, it was such a feline thing to do.

"If you're done playing!" I yelled, approaching with measured steps, a smile playing on my lips. I trusted my shifters to keep the other witches off me as I walked calmly toward the witch king. "I feel bad for Judah, Thorne. You've been trained better than to just harass your kills."

Thorne growled at me, flicking his tail in annoyance. I laughed. Judah simply stared, dumbfounded at the two of us. I stopped my forward momentum when I was only a few paces away.

"I apologize for the disrespect, King Judah. Thorne knows that he should just go in for the kill instead of messing around, but sometimes his feline nature gets the better of him." I tsked at the large sabertooth tiger.

"I'm going to—"

"What, Judah?" I interrupted his angry tirade. "You're going to do what exactly? Look around!" I held my arms out. "We're winning. So call everything off and talk to us like an adult."

Judah turned purple with anger. I popped my hip and crossed my arms over my chest, waiting. His eyes bounced around the battle before narrowing at what he was seeing. Malachi came to stand beside me, both of us studying the defeated witch.

I felt Judah gather his power an instant before he released it—a small, sharp soul dagger aimed right for me. A wall of earth rose quickly in front of me as I moved to dodge. I knew Ashera had blocked the blow with her elemental powers, and my relief was almost palpable.

A cold hand wrapped around my wrist and my eyes flashed to the perpetrator. *Ambrose.* Where the hell had he come from?

"Up you go, Your Majesty." With that, he threw me onto Judah's horse.

"Where the fuck have you been, you bloodsucking asshole?" I didn't hear Ambrose's response to Malachi's angrily shouted question.

I was too busy wrapping my arm around Judah's throat in a choke-hold and sliding a small dagger under his chin. The witch king stilled.

"Now I suggest you call off your underlings," I whispered in his ear.

"Where are you hiding your fae ally?" he hissed. "We were told Prince Caspian left Qamar."

My brain raced with the knowledge. There was a spy in our midst feeding information to our enemies. We'd suspected as much, but it still burned to have it confirmed. I chuckled, digging the blade in further. "You shouldn't believe everything you hear."

He stiffened before slowly shifting to raise a hand. I moved with him, never once easing my grip on him or my dagger. "Enough!" he called. "We've tested their strength. It is time we heard what Queen Winta and King Thorne have to say."

The witches immediately paused, confusion written all over their faces, but once they saw their king in my grasp, they instantly backed down, and my shifters followed suit.

My gaze shifted to Thorne, Ambrose, and Malachi. All three were covered in blood, looking smug.

"Only two of your guards may enter Qamar with you. The rest will remain out here." My voice rang out, and my shifters started to push the witches back away from the gates. "If anyone attempts to enter after us, all of you will be slaughtered. Am I clear?"

"Crystal," Judah snarled.

~

Thorne

WINTA ALWAYS TOOK ALL the fun away. Today with Judah was no different. I just wanted to toy with the stupid witch and make him squirm, maybe listen to him scream a bit. I wouldn't have hurt him all that much.

Ashera walked in front of Malachi and me, having come down from the tower now that all the commotion had ceased. Her little show of power back there had been hot as fuck. It had me wondering about all the kinky shit she liked to do in bed.

It bothered me that I couldn't see the glint of the sun on her hair or the sway of her pert ass as she walked. I couldn't see much of anything else for that matter because of the stupid fucking cloak she had to wear when she was out in public. My feline growled, wanting to see our mate just as much as I did.

My gaze traveled to Judah who was riding on his horse with Winta guiding the mount back to my house. It was the most secure place in the capital and our base if we couldn't be at the summer palace, which was a few hours away. We didn't want to leave the witch king out in the open for that long.

Winta and I had been fighting together in Qamar's army for a long time. I had known about her arranged marriage to Judah, but I hadn't thought twice about it. It was simply what royals did. Winta had seemed okay with it, so it wasn't my place to question it, but to watch him disrespect my queen like that... My skin rippled as I suppressed the shift. Rage wasn't the appropriate word. I would never tolerate anyone disrespecting Winta or Ashera in front of me. Ever.

Qamar was very much a patriarchal society, and women had always been viewed as second-class citizens. My grandparents had taken my mother in when my father had died in battle when I was just a toddler. My mother had made sure I knew how to treat a woman, and the bull-shit Judah just pulled out at the gates? My mother would have skinned him herself.

Winta had pulled the queen card, choosing to act diplomatically. At least she'd had a knife to the fucker's throat when she'd made her demand. I could respect her decision, especially in front of the others.

We needed to present ourselves as a united front, even if I'd fucked that up a bit by attacking first and asking questions after.

That was why I had hung back. Winta was much better at playing the diplomat, as was proven every time Judah glanced back at me and I gave him my best death glare and a low growl—not that he could hear me. His days were fucking numbered if I had anything to say about it.

"How many times do you plan on eye-fucking the witch?" Malachi bumped my shoulder with his.

"I'm not eye-fucking him," I growled. "I'm making sure he learns his godsdamned place."

The incubus threw his hands up with a grin. "Sure. But you should tell your dick to play along."

I glanced down at my body, which was still nude from when I'd shifted back. I'd been a bit rash and shredded my clothes in my rush to teach that fucking witch douche a lesson. Sure enough, my cock was standing at attention, and as soon as I noticed it, I felt the slam of arousal through my veins. *Shit, fuck, dammit.*

"I wish I could tell you this was for the witch jerkoff, but it's all for our little succubus mate up there." I pointed to where Ashera was walking with Ambrose. I could just make out the sway of her hips as she walked. Fuck, I wanted to be between those legs of hers way too much.

My dick grew impossibly harder as I imagined sinking into her warm, wet heat. It usually took the other women I'd been with a while to get used to my size, but I was sure Ashera would enjoy the challenge and adjust quickly. How long would it be before she'd let me take her ass? *Gods.* Mal glanced my way as I groaned aloud, picturing her lush ass slapping against my thighs as I drove in and out of her.

"Just mate with her already, cat boy," Mal muttered in exasperation.

I rolled my eyes. Bringing my attention back to the present, I focused on Judah in an attempt to ease my raging hard-on.

"First of all, I'm a sabertooth tiger. Not a cat. Second, you would really let me fuck Ashera? Just like that?" I didn't bother to hide the shock in my voice.

Malachi shrugged. "Ashera and I are both demons. We feed our magic through sexual energy. She's far more powerful than any other demon I've ever seen. She's going to need all the mates she can get to make sure she doesn't run out of power when she needs it.

"I fought the mate bond with her for a long time, and it wasn't healthy for either of us. When I finally came to my senses and accepted the bond, I knew I was going to have to accept any other mates that came her way. There was no way a female that powerful would be able to live off one mate. My only concern is that the idiots in her life treat her right. After watching the way you came to Winta's defense today... I'm not concerned."

For a male who had been one of the top assassins in the world, he was eerily laid back. It was possible I needed to sleep with one eye open from now on. Was this a trick? Was he going to beat me to a pulp the second I laid a finger on Ashera? I'd heard that harems in the other kingdoms often had hazing rituals. Was this one of those?

"Uh...Thanks," I said cautiously.

"Besides," he responded cheerfully, "it's not me you have to worry about." The demon tipped his chin toward Ashera, and I noticed Ambrose was walking backwards so he could give me a death glare. Ah, shit. Right. The vamp wasn't about to stop being a fucking douche.

I groaned again. Mating with Ashera was going to be an almost impossible mission—and this was without the fae in the picture. Between him and the vampire, I'd have to be as stealthy as possible.

Malachi laughed and nudged my shoulder. "Ambrose's bark is worse than his bite. He's just a bit insecure right now, and the whole Tomas situation has made any past insecurities he had a lot worse. Honestly, once you get it over with and mate with her, he'll calm down. You might lose some blood, but it's worth it."

It absolutely was. I squared my shoulders and pulled myself to my full height. Like I'd be afraid of a vamp, especially when it came to my mate. Fuck. That.

The sound of scrambling drew my attention to Winta and Judah. We'd made it back to my estate, and the soldiers and guards were scurrying around as Winta barked out orders on where to house Judah and how to ensure that those who were injured in the earlier fight were seen by a healer. I had no doubt Winta would house Judah in one of the guest rooms, even though I had perfectly acceptable, dank dungeons she could use. *Politics, gross.*

Malachi and I reached Ashera and Ambrose. "We'll wait for Winta in our room," Ashera said with a bright smile. She'd turned to face me as she spoke, and it was as though the sun was beaming out from behind a dark cloud. "I have a feeling she'll be with him for a while, so why don't we all have some food?"

"I can make that happen." I grinned down at her. She was such a petite thing, which was rare for demons. "Anything *else* you might desire?"

Ambrose snarled at me, slapping an icy hand against my chest. "We've got her desires covered, mutant."

Both Malachi and Ashera laughed and shook their heads while I rolled my eyes. Ambrose was going to have to get over the size difference. I was going to claim my mate. Period.

"Cool it." Ashera stabbed the cranky asshole with her finger. "Don't make me show you who the real dominant one is in this relationship, Ambrose."

The insecure prick's eyes heated, and he smirked down at our mate. "I think I might like that."

I wanted to gag.

"Come on, you two," Mal ordered as he ushered us all toward Ashera's bedchambers. "Princess, stop picking fights. Just because you have a smaller dick—"

"Let's not forget who got fucked with that dick, incubus," Ambrose growled.

I arched a brow. Really? The giant incubus assassin lost to the princess? I made a mental note to ask about that later. I needed to hear that story.

Malachi lashed out and slammed his fist into the side of the vamp's face. I choked back a laugh, but it burst free when I saw Ashera raise her hands as if asking for help from the gods.

"Will you two stop making a scene?" All heads whipped in my direction. "We're trying to keep Ashera safe, and you two are going to draw attention to us. At least wait until we're actually in Ashera's room before engaging in foreplay."

Ambrose mumbled something under his breath.

"What was that?" I asked.

"You're fucking right, you fucking pussy dick." I clenched my fists and took a deep breath. "We need to make sure that Ashera is safe, and we shouldn't have been reminded of that by a pussy."

I growled. I really, *really* wanted to break this asshole's face.

Once we were safely tucked inside Ashera's room, I couldn't take my eyes off my mate as she removed her cloak and stood before us without a top on. She was covered in blood and dried come. I blinked and then inhaled.

"What the actual *fuck?*" I yelled, spinning on Ambrose. It was his scent plastered all over her delicious body.

The cocky fucker just looked smug. "I made sure you would know your place."

My inner beast, already on a razor-thin edge because he wanted me to fuck Ashera into submission before claiming her, snarled. He viewed Ambrose as a threat to our mating and wanted me to rip him limb from limb before mounting our mate.

As though he sensed where my thoughts were heading—a naked Ashera screaming my name—Ambrose, the Prince of Tiny Penises, launched a fist at my face. I didn't evade the strike fast enough, and my head snapped back, my vision going blurry. I blinked down at my body as a heavy weight settled around my chest, arms, and legs. Chains. The fucker had somehow managed to magic chains around me.

"You don't get to fuck my mate with that abomination," Ambrose spat. I attempted to move, shift, something, but I couldn't. That bloodsucking fuckhead.

Weighed down and unable to move, I was forced to watch as Ambrose backed away with a shit-eating grin on his face. I wanted to punch that fucker into next week, wanted to turn the tables on him and make him watch as I fucked our mate in front of him. I was sure that was where this was going.

"I feel like another demonstration is in order, Mal. What do you think?" Our attention turned to the incubus, who was cleaning Ashera.

Malachi just shrugged in response. That asshole was going to go along with this? After everything he said outside? I was going to show all of them. I had a few surprises up my sleeve. If the vamp fucker thought my dick was intimidating now...

"Are we really going to do this again?" Malachi asked with a raised brow.

Again? What the fuck does that mean?

"Just like that fae fucker all over again." Ambrose chuckled. It was another story I would need to get out of these assholes.

"I'll allow it," Ashera inserted, "but only because I want to feed. Otherwise, I'd kick your ass, princess."

~

Ashera

I KNEW what Ambrose had planned. He wanted to make Thorne watch him and Mal fuck me until I forgot my name. I felt bad for Thorne, but I also knew if I stepped in too many times, the dynamic in my harem would be off and there would be infighting, so I needed to let them figure their shit out on their own. At least to a certain extent. If I thought Ambrose was going to take his issues with Thorne's delicious cock too far, I'd step in and make sure he remembered whose harem this was.

I was also curious to see how Thorne would react. Caspian, my violent and hostile fae, had been tense throughout the entire display put on by my other mates. Would Thorne be the same? I had a feeling that my feline shifter mate would roll with the punches much better than Caspian.

I'd been paying too much attention to Thorne and failed to notice Malachi come up behind me, his chest flush against my back as his hand wrapped around my throat. His erection pressed against me, so I pushed against him harder.

"Uh-uh, my little slut," he whispered in my ear. "You aren't in control right now. I am."

A shiver ran down my spine. His tone was deep and husky, dark. It was a zap of electricity right to my clit. I loved it when Malachi talked dirty and called me his little slut. This strong, deadly assassin wanted me so much, he broke all the rules for me, and that caused heat to pool in my core.

"Yes, sir," I replied in a teasing tone.

Malachi answered with a low growl that had me moaning. "Watch what you say, Sher. You'll need to call me sir from here on out if you don't."

The thought had me dripping. "Understood, Sir."

Ambrose appeared in front of me, clearly not wanting to be forgotten. I hated to admit that for a second there, I *had* forgotten he was in the room with us. Malachi made it so easy to fall into him, for it to be him and only him. My rock.

Dropping to his knees, Ambrose slowly trailed his gaze up my body, igniting every inch it landed on. Mal's grip tightened around my neck, and his other hand curled around my breast to pinch my nipple. I rested my head against his chest.

My mates shredded the leathers until I was bare before them. Thorne growled low in his throat, but I didn't hear him attempt to move, and I was too over stimulated to lift my head to check on him.

"Princess Ambrose is going to eat your tight little pussy before he feeds off you, slut." Malachi started to pinch my nipple again. "Then we're going to fight over who gets to fill that little pussy and who gets to come down your throat."

"I want her ass." Ambrose pouted up at us.

"It won't make for the greatest show for the cat, but fine, we'll fight over who gets to fuck your ass." Malachi chuckled, and I moaned. "But first, princess, you're going to make Ashera come on your tongue and fingers before giving a taste to the pussy who's all tied up."

I didn't care who touched me, I just needed to be touched right fucking now. Mal's words had me so wound up, it wouldn't take much for me to go off like a damn rocket.

Ambrose lifted my legs so my thighs rested on his shoulders and his face was in prime pussy eating position. A small whine from Thorne broke my concentration for a moment, but Ambrose decided that was the right moment to dive right in.

Mal braced me against his chest, using the grip on my throat and the hand around my waist to hold me in place. Ambrose grasped my ass while his fingers fluttered against my opening. His damn tongue was circling my clit, causing my hips to buck against him. He was teasing me.

"Stay still, little slut," Malachi murmured against my ear. "I don't want to have to punish you."

"Whatever the fuck you just said to her, keep it up, Bat Fuck. She's almost fucking drowning me." Ambrose went back to teasing my clit as his fingers skimmed over my soaked slit, and my incubus released a dark chuckle.

Two slender digits worked their way into my core right as lush lips closed around my clit and sucked hard. The fingers inside me curled to hit my G-spot, and I came with a scream so loud, I would be surprised if Malachi wasn't deaf by the end of this. Ambrose didn't let up. He kept sucking on my clit and working my G-spot, and I just kept coming.

"Good girl," Malachi crooned against my ear. "Keep coming around your princess's fingers just like that."

He released his pheromones, and spots swam in my vision. I distantly heard Thorne's roar, no doubt finding his own release thanks to all of the sex flooding the air.

Ambrose removed his fingers mere moments before he sank his fangs into my thigh. I groaned, clenching my legs around his head. I was sure if I was hurting him, he would stop me, so I just squeezed and rode the wave.

Malachi ripped me from my vampire, threw me on the bed, and then tackled the shit out of Ambrose. His fist landed squarely on Ambrose's jaw just as a knee landed on the vampire's ribs. I winced. That had to hurt.

"Do you want to know a secret, you bloodsucking douchebag?" Malachi sneered as he wrestled a squirming Ambrose into a choke hold.

Ambrose cursed and attempted to buck the incubus off him, but it was no use. Malachi had him pinned.

"I let you win last time." My thighs clenched at this. "I let you fuck my ass. Do you want to know why?"

I sure as fuck wanted to know.

"Because I knew my little slut would love every minute of watching you fuck me, but I get her ass, princess. You get what I give you." He smashed another fist into Ambrose's face.

My gaze finally flicked over to Thorne to find his gaze glued to my fighting mates. His facial features shifted quickly, a clear sign that he was about to lose control over his animal, but those magical chains weren't going anywhere. Not without Ambrose taking them off of him.

Thorne's gaze slid to me, and I gasped at the hunger there. I knew if he was given the chance, he would devour me in a heartbeat. I wanted it, but not without all of my mates in agreement first. His eyes flicked between his normal eyes and the eyes of his feline.

"When I fuck you, Ashera," Thorne growled, "I'm going to make them watch as my come drips out of your pussy, then I'm going to make that fanged fucker lick it out of you."

Ambrose growled at that, but he didn't say anything against the idea. A small moan escaped me, and my thighs clenched, the visual doing all the right things to heat my blood. I needed at least one of my mates inside me immediately.

Malachi stood with his arm around Ambrose's neck, keeping a firm grip on my squirming vampire. I shuffled over to one side of the bed before Mal pushed Ambrose down on his back. He positioned the vamp in such a way that Thorne would have a clear view of me sandwiched between my two large mates, but he wouldn't get to see much else. It seemed as though it wasn't just me they wanted to tease tonight.

"If you shift in those chains, I will choke you with my cock, is that clear?" Malachi snarled at Thorne. A quick glance told me he was still struggling to control his shift, and a low growl was his only response.

Taking that as acquiescence, my assassin then turned to me, grabbed my waist, and settled me so I was straddling Ambrose. My breath caught in my throat. There was something so delicious about a man who could manhandle me like that.

"Now sink that sweet little pussy down on the vampire's cock like the good slut you are." Malachi's deep, husky voice had me shuddering and moving quickly to obey him.

"Yes, Sir." I sank down onto Ambrose's cock, relishing the soft curse he muttered as I did so.

I could hear Mal digging around in the nightstand before the soft pop of the lube bottle filled the silence. My pussy fluttered around Ambrose at the thought of taking both of them. I loved when my mates filled me at the same time and we were able to all be connected in some way.

Thorne's growls increased in volume as my incubus slid into my ass. I couldn't hold back my gasp of pleasure when Ambrose and Mal were both seated inside me. None of my mates lacked in size, and it was always interesting when they decided to take me together like this. I was curious about taking Thorne and one of my other mates. Mal was probably the second biggest, possibly Caspian.

"Holy fuck." Ambrose groaned. "What are you thinking about, little queen?"

Answering him would only piss him off, so I didn't. Instead, I leaned down and allowed my fangs to drop. Malachi thrust into me as my fangs penetrated Ambrose's neck. All three of us moaned, while Thorne continued growling across the room.

Ambrose's hips moved against mine as I started to rock against them, taking them deeper with each downward thrust of my hips. The metallic tang of blood burst on my tongue as I sipped from my vampire mate, his power filling me.

Malachi released another surge of pheromones as his hand landed against my ass with a crack. I ripped my lips from Ambrose's neck as my back arched and a ragged breath left my lungs.

"Feed off us," Malachi demanded, and I obeyed.

My mates took over our movements. Mal gripped my hips tightly as they started to slam into me, releasing low growls. I reattached my mouth to the wound on my vamp's neck.

Feeding off both blood and sexual energy made my head spin, and my pleasure spiraled out of control. Distantly, I could feel my pleasure weave its way through all of the mates I'd formed bonds with. Winta, now alone in a bathroom, was panting on the floor as her release barreled ever closer. Caspian and Jacobi had their pants around their knees in a wooded area, stroking their cocks as they raced to their own orgasms. My vampire and incubus were struggling to stay in control long enough to make me shatter around them.

"Feed off her, Ambrose." Malachi cursed as I clamped around them. "And make sure to get that clit so she can strangle our cocks."

Ambrose nuzzled his face against my neck as his fingers started to gently circle my clit. I moaned around his throat, then screamed as his fangs sank into my flesh. I felt all of my mates release at the same time, making my orgasm stronger, and I came so hard, dark spots flickered around my vision. Malachi and Ambrose were both pulled over the edge with me, snarling out their releases in tandem.

A feral sounding roar had me looking over at Thorne, my chest heaving with harsh pants as I tried to regain control of myself. He was half shifted, his eyes completely feline as he watched us come down from our highs. His chest rose and fell with each savage pull of oxygen into and out of his lungs, and his stomach was splashed with his own release.

"I'm going to fill you up so much you'll be dripping for a week," he snarled at me. "I won't let you out of that fucking bed until your precious *princess* of a mate cleans it all off with his tongue. Once that's done, I'm going to come on your tits, your ass, and your face, and let your other mates lick those areas clean. Make no mistake, little mate, by the time I'm done with you, you'll know damn well that you belong to *me*."

6

CASPIAN

The feathered fuck and I had been minding our own damn business, walking as silently as we could in the forest that bordered Qamar and Malak, when the first wave of Ashera's arousal hit us. We'd decided it was the safest, though not the fastest route to Juniya. We couldn't be entirely sure what we'd run into during our trip, and we wanted to remain as incognito as possible.

"I'd gotten a small amount of arousal earlier, but this..." Jacobi panted, reaching out to plant a palm on a nearby tree for balance.

I doubled over at the next wave. *Fuck.* I reached out to steady myself against the same tree. Whatever they were doing to our mate... A shudder slammed through my body, and I groaned.

"Are they—" I groaned again. "Fucking her to within an inch of her life?"

I could barely get the question out before another shudder ran through me. I glanced at Jacobi. He wasn't fairing much better. In fact, he was already digging into his pants to release his straining cock. Smart fucker. I started to do the same.

Our chests rose and fell with each harsh breath we took, focusing on the arousal and lust. Whatever they were doing to our sweet mate, she was *invested*.

"I'm going to fucking kill them for this," I growled as I fisted my cock.

The need for release was almost blinding. All I could feel was Ashera's desire through our bond, and all I could hear was the gentle slaps as Jacobi and I jerked off. Fuck, I could practically smell Ashera's sweet pussy.

Thankfully, as quickly as the lust and arousal slammed into us, our releases weren't far behind, blasting through us in time with our mate's. Both of us sagged against the tree we'd been leaning on. Our shoulders touched, but I didn't give a fuck. My lungs screamed for air, my legs shook, and my heart felt as though it was about to pound its way out of my fucking chest.

I glanced down at myself in disgust. I was covered in my own come... again. This was becoming a habit with our little merry band of assholes—one I didn't exactly appreciate. I grumbled as I used a small amount of magic to clean myself off before I pulled my pants back up, glancing over at Jacobi once I was finished.

The angel king was flushed, his chest still heaving at a rapid rate, but he'd cleaned himself up and had his pants secured around his hips again. Good. I had no issue seeing the others' cocks when we were pleasuring our mate, but when it was just the two of us, I'd rather he kept that to himself.

"I know she needs to feed," he said, "but gods."

I understood the feeling. I rubbed my hands down my face before gesturing for us to continue our journey. I was a bit too irritated to engage in chitchat about what had just happened. Hell, I was still rock hard. Frustrated didn't even begin to cover how I felt.

I wanted to be back in Qamar with my mate. I wanted to be there while they tortured and teased her. Feeling everything from the outside like this sucked. It was... lonely. I cursed quietly under my breath. Ashera had turned us into total and complete saps. I'd deny it until my death, but I wouldn't have it any other way.

I hadn't realized how hard being away from her would be. I hadn't thought I would struggle to put one foot in front of the other as I made my way away from her. How the fuck could I have initially thought I'd be able to just walk away from her? I'd been a damn fool.

"Malachi must have been bossing her around," I joked in a poor attempt to lighten the mood. Jacobi seemed to be just as wound up as I was. "She always loves it when one of us takes charge."

The angel king chuckled, but the sound lacked any humor. He was just as ruined as the rest of us when it came to the petite succubus who had tied us all together. We both wanted to be back with her, and what just happened had highlighted just how difficult this actually was for us. I was curious if this was just as hard for her.

With several mates to keep Ashera busy, did she feel our absence just as keenly as we felt hers?

I shook off the thought. I couldn't dwell on shit like that right now. I needed to focus on getting to Juniya and confronting my father. Concentrating on how it felt as though I was missing a limb because I wasn't by Ashera's side would only cause me to fuck this entire mission straight to hell. There was too much riding on us for me to get this wrong.

"How do you think this is going to go?" Jacobi asked, pulling my attention out of my depressing thoughts. "Are we going to need to fight our way out of Juniya?"

I glanced at the sky as I pondered his question. The sun had started to paint it with stunning pinks and purples as it began to sink beyond the horizon. The fact that Jacobi had even bothered to ask told me he didn't know my father as well as he should. That, and he was far too hopeful that my father wasn't a complete asshole.

I sort of felt bad telling him the truth.

Malak had always been an anomaly in Dunya. They'd never owned slaves and had always seemed to live in peace with every other king-dom. Their reputation in the other kingdoms was fair, albeit a little stuck-up. I hadn't been surprised to learn that Jacobi, their king, had shown up alone to greet the new Queen of Shaytan. It was an unspoken rule that Malak and its leaders were respected as neutral in all things.

Knowing that Jacobi was willing to go to war for Ashera spoke volumes about the mate bond, yet I knew it was more than that. Jacobi wasn't going to sign his peaceful kingdom up for war just for his mate. He was doing it because he realized—like I had—that staying silent about the issue only perpetuated it. You weren't innocent when you sat by and watched atrocities happen, you were complacent. You still had blood on your hands, especially if you were in a position to do something about it and turned the other way.

I believed that was why I'd pushed back so hard when I'd first become Ashera's mate. I hadn't made her any false promises, and I hadn't actually intended on changing my mind. I hadn't wanted to face the fact that I was wrong... that I'd been complacent. Worse, in some ways, I'd been an active participant. She'd opened my eyes to all of it. She'd made me realize that in many cases, doing nothing was just as wrong as being an instigator.

She'd taught me that as a prince, I had the power to change things, and not just for the people of Juniya. I owed her more than I could fathom.

I glanced at Jacobi. "I won't lie to you, we might have to fight." I sighed. "My father is... difficult. Difficult and stubborn. Getting him to agree to something like this..." I shook my head. "I don't have any illusions that this is going to go smoothly."

Jacobi studied me for a moment before he nodded. "Okay. So how do we want to play this then?"

"Just let me do most of the talking," I replied. It was the best we could do.

We had to make a small camp that night, as it was too dark to continue on. In the morning, I was grudgingly making my way along before I stopped, almost causing Jacobi to trip over himself. "Why the fuck are we walking? You've got wings."

Laughter burst out of Jacobi as he rolled his eyes at me. "I wasn't about to offer to carry you around like some damsel in distress. But if you'd rather fly, I have no objections to getting us to your father faster. It means returning to Ashera sooner."

I huffed and glared at the feathered fuck. I had to ask him? I wanted to strangle him. "Well, don't just stand there, you birdbrained asshole. Let's get a move on!"

With a soft chuckle, Jacobi picked me up and took flight. I attempted to maintain some semblance of dignity throughout this process.

Soon, we were flying high over the forest, edging ever closer to the mountains that ran through Sahira, Masas, Malak, and Juniya. The forests bordering the mountains were flanked by green meadows with shifters tending to small flocks of sheep and goats on the flower dotted hills. It would have made for a lovely painting, a still life of peace and prosperity.

The green hills turned rocky, and the shepherds disappeared as we made our way into the mountains, the natural border between Qamar and Juniya. It was the largest mountain range in Dunya, with peaks so high they were impassable. They also held valuable resources for my people.

The fae were farmers, harvesting the vegetables and fruits for all of Dunya, and the mountains provided an endless source of spring water for our crops, which we harnessed into sprinkler systems, utilizing Juniya's moderate year-round weather to maintain maximum crop yields. Juniya was lucky. We framed the southern edge of Dunya and had temperate weather all year, and this allowed us to rotate our crops so we never had fallow fields. Our elemental powers aided us in keeping the soil fertile, plants healthy, and springs full.

Juniya's capital, Mazraea, was in a valley at the foot of the mountains and had a river running through its heart. With our elemental magic, we used the land around us to our advantage, which meant it was an easily defendable position—one we'd never given up in the entire history of our people. The castle at the heart of the city was a sprawling mess of a structure and designed to touch at least part of every element a fae could control. I'd learned to harness my own powers on this land, as had all fae for centuries. Every fae could control at least one element, learning and practicing enough to gain total mastery over it. Stronger fae could control two or possibly three.

The thought of the city's defenses had me frowning. I knew Juniya's defenses, military strategies, and where key targets were if this came to a fight with my father. Could I really do that to the people? Could their prince willingly slaughter them? I didn't have an answer, and for the first time in my long life, I actually prayed to the gods that I wouldn't need to come up with one. I could control five elements—

earth, air, fire, metal, and water—and had no interest in turning that power on my people. Not unless I was forced to.

I needed to focus on the points I'd make to my father. Ashera was counting on me to make this work. Gods. This was a futile mission, but Ashera had asked. How could I possibly refuse her?

"We've crossed into Juniya," Jacobi called over the wind. I nodded, gesturing for us to touch down. I didn't want to cause the patrols undue alarm. This was a delicate situation, and I didn't need us getting shot out of the damn sky.

As our feet touched the ground, I could hear the pounding of footsteps approach us. Just as I'd suspected, the patrol had come to investigate rather than run off to warn others, which was what I wanted to avoid. That would have caused panic and pissed off my father, making this worse than it already was.

"Halt!" a fae male yelled as he and three others approached. "Halt in the name of King Ivan!"

I allowed them to get close enough to get a good look at my face. When they realized who I was, they paled. They paled even further when they got a good look at Jacobi. Malak and Juniya traded often, so there was no mistaking the angel king.

"Y-Your Highness! Your Majesty!" All the men in the patrol bowed. "Please forgive us! We didn't know you would be crossing the border!"

Jacobi remained silent, for which I was immensely thankful. "At ease. I apologize for not sending word ahead of time, but there is an urgent matter I wished to discuss with my father. We landed as soon as we crossed the border so as not to cause alarm."

"Of course, Your Highness!" The male's gaze kept bouncing between me and Jacobi. "Do you require an escort, Your Highness?"

"No." I shook my head. "Please head back to your duties."

They all bowed and scrambled to get away. They must be fairly new recruits if being around royals rattled them this much.

"They'll send word that we're on our way." I turned to look at the angel king. "We might as well fly the rest of the way to Mazraea."

∾

Malachi

IF IT HAD BEEN UP to me, I probably wouldn't have engaged in quite a show of dominance in front of Thorne. I almost liked the shifter—well, more so than I had liked the fae or vampire when they'd first shown up. Thorne had Ashera's best interests at heart, and I would never deny her more mates. I'd been honest when I'd spoken to Thorne about it. As powerful as she was, and with her powers in flux right now, she needed as many mates as she could get to keep her well-fed.

I glanced at the vampire curled around my Sher. Ambrose seemed rather insistent that we show Thorne who Ashera's "real" mates were. The poor guy had been having such a hard time, so I didn't have the heart to deny him a moment of security. At least not right now. He'd have to work it through with Ashera and Thorne.

I sat on the edge of the bed, glancing at my mate and her vampire again. They were both snoring softly as they slept. We'd released Thorne from his restraints last night and sent him on his way after he'd calmed down enough not to rip the fanged fucker to shreds. I had a sneaking suspicion he'd be banging on our door any minute now.

After standing and stretching, I made my way over to the bathroom for a quick scrub down. Once I made sure that Thorne wasn't about to cause a bloodbath this morning, I wanted to hunt Winta down. She'd had plenty of time with Judah, and if she hadn't been able to get through to him, it was my turn to try.

I was just pulling on my pants, with Ambrose and Ashera starting to stir in bed, when Thorne burst through the door. His chest heaved as he studied our mate and her vampire, who were sleepily blinking up at him. I moved to stand at the foot of the bed, close enough so I could kick the fucker out if I needed to, but still out of the way so they could all work this out without me.

Thorne opened his mouth, shook his head, and then closed it. I chuckled.

"I did warn you," I said, drawing his attention away from the couple in bed. "You two are going to need to work out your issues."

"Soon would be nice," Ashera interjected with a yawn.

Silence rang around the room as we all watched her stretch, the sheet falling to her waist to display her perfect pert breasts. My cock stirred in my pants. No. Bad. Now was not the time.

"Why don't you take a quick shower, Sher?" I helped her out of bed and pointed her in the direction of the bathroom. "I'm going to put these two assholes in their place."

"Thank you. I love you." She leaned up on her tiptoes to press a quick kiss to my lips. My heart lurched as I grinned down at her.

Once the door was closed behind Ashera, I spun to face Thorne and Ambrose. "I'm going to go talk to Winta and see about Judah. I think the two of you should beat the shit out of each other. It'll make you both feel better."

Ambrose growled and didn't move from his spot in the bed, while Thorne just shrugged. I wanted to bash their brains in myself. Idiots. I was surrounded by idiots.

"What room does Winta have Judah in?" I asked.

"He's in the other wing. Winta didn't want him too close to Ashera," Thorne informed me, and then he gave me directions.

I nodded in thanks. "Seriously. You two need to work this shit out. Ambrose, if I need to beat you again, I am more than happy to do it. But stop torturing Ashera by not allowing her to finalize her bond with Thorne. You're being a shitty mate.

I left the two of them in silence and made my way to the other wing of Thorne's estate. Ashera was more than capable of putting two stupid males in their place if she needed to. I also couldn't be there to force any sort of resolution between the three of them, because it wouldn't last, but it was damn hard to walk away from my mate when there were two morons fighting over her.

I was thankful that whoever designed Thorne's house hadn't felt the need to make it a maze of random hallways. It was very easy to get from one room to another without getting lost, so when I finally walked up to the door to Judah's room, I paused before knocking. I almost wanted to burst out laughing. Winta had put Judah in the servants' quarters. I had no doubt the witch king loathed the very thought.

I pounded my fist against the door twice before Winta's voice rang out. "Who is it?"

"It's Mal." There was a pause, and then the door opened just the slightest bit and Winta peered out.

"What do you want?"

"I came to talk to Judah."

She huffed and narrowed her eyes. "I can handle this."

"Of that I have no doubt, Your Majesty," I replied. "But as Shaytan's king, I'd like to sit down with King Judah. Everything we have to say to him concerns all three kingdoms, so it's best if I am here to accurately represent Shaytan."

She stared at me for a moment before nodding and fully opening the door. "Of course, I apologize, King Malachi."

Those two words had me cringing inside. I was no king, regardless of what Ashera or the rest of Dunya thought. I entered Judah's quarters and once again had to hold back my laughter. It was tiny, only big enough to hold little more than a small bed and wardrobe. It certainly wasn't a room fit for royalty. He must be fuming.

And yet, by looking at him, I couldn't tell if he was ruffled at all. It was such a contrast to yesterday's childish display of anger. Once more, something felt off about him, causing my focus to narrow on him entirely. I needed to discover what he was hiding in order to keep Ashera safe.

I shuffled over to stand in front of the wardrobe, giving Winta enough room to stand directly in front of Judah who sat on the bed.

"You expect me to believe that you came here simply to talk, demon?" Judah spat at me. "How stupid do you think I am?"

"I really shouldn't answer that, Your Majesty," I answered with a smirk. His cheeks darkened, and his eyes heated with hatred. "However, I did come here just to talk to you."

"I've informed him of the events in Qamar leading up to the revolution against my father," Winta informed me. "You've actually come at just the right time."

"Indeed." Judah sighed. "You're to tell me how aiding the resistance against your little dead succubus is wrong, how slavery is bad, and how we can all be best friends and go skipping into the sunset."

I pinched the bridge of my nose and closed my eyes. Was I cursed to deal with childish males for the rest of my life? Gods, I hoped not.

"No. I'm here to explain how things are going to work. You're going to tell us what we need to know about the resistance. If you don't cooperate with us..." I shrugged. "We'd planned to invade Sahira anyway."

Judah laughed. "Invade Sahira? Do tell. Without Masas on your side, there's no way you could possibly enter my kingdom without massive losses."

He wasn't wrong. While we could enter through Malak, the two kingdoms shared a very small border that was made up of a dangerous mountain range that ran along the coast. I was sure we'd be able to use Malak's ships to get to Sahira, but the oceans around Dunya were dangerous unless navigated by an expert captain. There wouldn't be enough people to captain a fleet large enough to get the necessary soldiers to Sahira. Masas was the easiest means of invasion.

Without Ambrose there to take control away from Tomas...

"Ambrose is the rightful King of Masas," Winta responded.

"I imagine Tomas has a thing or two to say about that," Judah taunted.

"I'm sure he does," I replied. "Too bad the coward isn't here to face his son like a man. Instead, we have to chase him like an errant child."

Judah glared at me.

"How long has Sahira been helping Tomas with the resistance?" I asked. "Have you always been in bed with him?"

The witch king scoffed. "Sahira and Masas have always been close allies. I never said that I was aiding the resistance."

"You didn't have to." I smirked at him. "There were witches in the hinterlands of Masas during the attack that killed Queen Ashera."

"At least not all of my people are worthless." Gods, I wanted to break this fucker's nose. "Though I'm sure there are demons and shifters in this resistance as well, and yet neither of you approve such behavior. Am I to be held accountable for the misdeeds of some of my people?"

"No," Winta cut in. "But you are to explain your behavior and give us all the information you can on Tomas's whereabouts. After all, Sahira and Qamar are still close allies as well, correct?"

I quirked a brow at the queen. She was good.

"Of course, of course!" Judah agreed. "Can't very well say that we aren't allies when you have me locked in this sad excuse of a house, now can I?"

"So talk," I commanded.

"You know," the annoying asshole drawled, "I don't think I'm going to. You see, you're consorting with the fae to overthrow both Masas and Sahira over a *woman*. What allegiance do I really owe any of you?"

I pulled Winta over to the door and leaned down to whisper into her ear. "Go get your mate. Have her stand outside the door and pull. She'll know what to do."

Winta looked at me with questioning eyes, but I nodded. She shrugged and left the room.

"Gone for backup?" Judah goaded with a grin playing on his lips. "The infamous incubus assassin can't get the soft witch king to crack and needs reinforcements?"

I chuckled. "You think we're consorting with the fae. Whatever gave you that idea?"

Judah shot me a look that suggested I was dumber than a rock. "I don't know. Maybe the wall of earth that shot up in front of Winta. No other creature can do that except a fae, and we all know that Juniya's prince stood up as one of the succubus's mates. Tell me, did you kill Ivan to get the fae to help you with this stupid mission of yours?"

So Juniya wasn't involved with the resistance. I was fairly certain that Judah, and thereby Sahira, was involved with Tomas and his rogue vampires. We hadn't been entirely sure about Caspian's father, however.

"If she were still alive, I'd offer myself up as a mate," Judah continued, unaware of my thoughts. "Seems as though she's collecting one from every kingdom, and Sahira is the last one left. Such a shame she'll never be able to have witch cock."

My entire body went rigid, and I immediately fell back into my assassin training. My fists clenched at my sides as I took a few calming breaths. It wouldn't do to strangle the annoying fucker here, not until we knew for sure that killing him was in our best interests long term. He was digging for information just as much as we were, I could see that plain as day. I just needed to figure out exactly what I wanted to feed him.

Even if he offered up information after Ashera took a sip from his powers, I wasn't about to trust him. There were too many red flags.

Winta entered the room a moment later, closing the door behind her. She grinned up at me, her eyes dancing. Ashera must have explained what I had planned on the way over.

"Now, King Judah," Winta began, "I know this transition can't be easy on you. After all, you lost your future wife and a potential second kingdom all in one day. But I implore you to see reason."

I could feel the pull of Ashera's powers as she started to drain Judah. It was clear, at first, he had no idea what was going on. The witch king looked around the room in confusion. The more Ashera pulled from him, the more frantic he became until he finally shot to his feet.

"Enough! What's going on?" Judah yelled. Ashera stopped draining him. "You will explain what the fuck is going on right this moment."

"Funny." I chuckled. "You're not exactly in a position to be making demands." I stepped in front of him. "Now sit down and answer us." I pushed him back onto the bed.

~

Caspian

WE WERE FINALLY inside Mazraea's palace, our footsteps echoing down the hallway as we made our way to my father's private study. I was surprised to discover that my heart was pounding out an unsteady rhythm in my chest, pushing so hard against my ribs it felt as though the organ would burst through my rib cage, splatter on the floor, and sputter off down the hall.

"I never expected you to feel nervous," Jacobi murmured.

My brain froze, stuttering to a complete standstill even though my legs continued to move. *Nervous?* I wanted to scoff. There was no way I was nervous. What the fuck did I have to be nervous about? Only the fate of my entire kingdom, my mate's life, the possibility that I would need to kill my father, and the wellbeing of every being in Dunya. It could all be lost in a war that could so easily be avoided if we all just got our heads out of our asses for once.

There was absolutely *nothing* to be nervous about.

I was calm and collected.

I turned to glare at Jacobi. "I'm not nervous."

He raised a brow at me. "I'm an empath. Nice try."

Fucking-feathered-fucker-fucking-fuck.

"Right. Still not nervous." I rolled my eyes, fighting the urge to punch the winged asshole.

"Whatever you say." Jacobi shrugged.

I stopped us outside of an inconspicuous wooden door. This study was my father's sanctuary, and he didn't want to blast its whereabouts to everyone in the palace. It was the one place he truly got to be alone. Not that he was able to use it much. It was also the only place we'd ever have private meetings together.

I glanced over at Jacobi again. "Just hang back and let me handle this."

"I'm here to support you, Caspian," he replied. "I have no interest in coming between you and your father. If you need my help, you only need to ask for it."

Strangely, I appreciated that. I straightened my spine, took one last deep breath, and pushed the door open. There was no reason to knock. He knew we were in the palace and coming to see him. Knocking suggested a form of respect I didn't have for the old man, so I wanted to make sure he knew where he stood with me.

"Caspian!" My father's jovial voice carried across the study, and I froze in the doorway. My mother sat on my father's desk, facing him, with her legs braced on either side of him. What the fuck was going on?

"Caspian, dear!" My mother turned her head to look over at me, a bright smile appearing on her face. "I'm so pleased you're home!"

Jacobi coughed into his hand to hide his shock. Meanwhile, I just stood there like an idiot with my mouth hanging open as I stared at my parents as though I'd never seen them before in my life.

In a way, I hadn't. I'd never seen them like this before. I knew my parents cared for one another, theirs had been a lucky love match, something most royals never got. But I'd *never* seen them so... I shuddered. No. I didn't want to think about what they'd been doing before we'd come into the room. Nope. Gross.

Once my brain finally processed what I was seeing, and I acknowledged I'd possibly need to down some poison to get the image out of my mind, I made my way into the study and sat on the chair opposite my father's desk. Jacobi stepped inside, closing the door behind him.

My mother shimmied until she was sitting in my father's lap, facing the room. I held back a gag.

"Son, I'm pleased you've come home. We have much to discuss." My father wrapped his arms around my mother's waist as he talked.

My eyes bounced between the two of them. "Like this?" I asked, gesturing to them.

My father's gaze hardened. "Caspian, I've indulged your narrow-minded bullshit for too long."

I didn't think him breaking my nose could have shocked me more in that moment. He had indulged my narrow-minded bullshit? He was the one who had taught me the bullshit in the first place! Once again, my brain short-circuited and my mouth hung open.

"Dear," my mother chided, "close your mouth. King Jacobi will assume we didn't teach you any manners at all!"

"I'm sorry." I held up my hand. "I just want to be clear. *My* narrow-minded bullshit?"

The smug look that crossed my father's face was infuriating enough that I was surprised they couldn't see steam coming out of my ears.

"Ever since we hired that tutor—what the hell was his name?" My father paused to think. "It doesn't matter. You've assumed so many things."

"What things?" I yelled.

Jacobi's light cough behind me jerked me back to the real reason we were here. Whatever the hell was going on with my father could wait —this portion of it anyway.

"Right." I sighed, running my hands over my hair. "That's not why we're here."

"And why are you here, Caspian?" My father's voice held a hint of menace to it. He was never a fan of being ignored or denied his fun.

"We're here to discuss slavery and get troops to aid in our fight against the resistance." I kept my tone calm and controlled.

"Slavery and the resistance... Riveting conversation, son." My father arched a brow before gesturing for me to continue.

This whole situation had put me off-kilter, so I wasn't entirely sure how I wanted to start this discussion. I forced down the urge to turn to look at Jacobi for help. This was my battle. I'd made that clear. I also wanted my father to respect me.

"Slavery in Juniya ends now," I stated with far more confidence and authority than I felt.

"Done," my father responded instantly.

"I'm sorry... What?" I knew I was yelling again, but what the hell did they expect?

Jacobi moved to stand beside me, just as invested in the answer as I was. We were both staring at my parents in shock.

"We've been in the process of freeing all the slaves in Juniya for the past twenty years, Caspian." My father waved his hand in front of his face as though this was old news. "Our economy needed time to adjust. We're about to commence the last stages. This is an easy thing to agree to."

"Why wasn't I informed?" I demanded.

"You're an asshole," my father deadpanned.

My mother shot him a scathing look over her shoulder. "What your father *meant* to say..." She paused and studied my face. "Caspian, you've become stuck in your ways, too blinded by your own thoughts to see what's going on around you. You think that you know best, and that's that."

I sucked in a breath. This wasn't easy to hear, and a part of me wanted to argue, but hadn't Ashera and I had similar conversations about how I was? I'd done this to myself.

"That is good to hear," Jacobi murmured. "Not that Caspian is an asshole, though I already knew that, but that Juniya has been freeing its slaves. We were unaware that you'd initiated such a program."

"Yes, well..." My father coughed slightly. "My wife made a very valid point during a discussion, and we implemented plans shortly thereafter."

My father actually listened to my mother? Would the surprises never end?

Sensing my need for introspection, Jacobi continued his discussion with my father. "As for the resistance, we plan on meeting an army at Sahira, where we have every reason to believe King Tomas of Masas is hiding. He is, to the best of our knowledge, the leader of the resistance against Queen Ashera. We need additional soldiers to aid us in the fight."

"You speak as though Queen Ashera is still alive," my mother commented.

Jacobi and I locked gazes. It would be a risk to tell my parents that Ashera was, in fact, still alive. They didn't seem to side with the resistance, but could we trust them with our mate's life? I was so jumbled right now, given all I'd learned, that I didn't know, so I nodded to Jacobi, hoping he understood that I would trust him if he wanted to explain.

With a nod of his own, Jacobi turned back to my parents, studying them intently for a moment before speaking. "Ashera is your son's mate. Mine as well. She's still alive, though she was greatly wounded in Masas. We're keeping this knowledge secret in an attempt to flush out the resistance. We want to eradicate any threat to her as quickly as possible."

My parents glanced at each other before studying us. The silence seemed to stretch on forever, making my skin itch. I had to fight the urge to twitch as we all regarded one another.

"Take as many soldiers as you need," my father finally said. "Juniya's resources are yours, son."

I damn near collapsed in relief.

～

Winta

WE'D LEFT Judah in the room I'd assigned him a few hours ago with guards stationed in the hallway and outside the windows. He'd been willing to listen as we fed him strategic lies about the elemental magic he'd seen. We'd given him his options—join us or remain imprisoned until we could hunt down Tomas—and left to let him think about things.

I knew Malachi wouldn't trust Judah no matter what he said now that he had all the information we were willing to give him. Not that I could blame him. I wasn't entirely sure I'd be able to trust Judah either. There was still a small spark of hope he'd show me he was still the young witch I knew as a child, but that ship was quickly sailing, leaving me with a broken heart over a lost friendship.

I found Ashera sitting in Thorne's study, somehow alone, with a small stack of papers on the desk in front of her. Thorne's study here was small in comparison to the one at the summer palace. It had a large fireplace that dominated most of the wall to the right of the door that was framed with bookshelves. More shelves lined the wall opposite the fireplace. Ashera's back was to a wall of windows that looked out over the forest that surrounded Thorne's estate. There were two large leather chairs that stood in front of the currently empty fireplace and a desk with a chair. That was it.

It was simple, and so unlike the man who often used this space.

"I'm surprised to find you alone," I remarked with a grin when Ashera looked up to see that I was leaning against the closed study door. "Your vampire doesn't seem to want to let you out of his sight, and Thorne takes far too much pleasure in tormenting him."

Ashera laughed, the musical sound filling my soul with a peace I'd never been able to find before her. I didn't care that I was her reincarnated mate. All I cared about was that she was here, safe, whole, and mine. My dragon rumbled in agreement at the thought. She was perfect for us, and we were so blessed by the gods that we'd been able to find her.

I'd always been more attracted to women than men, but I hadn't wanted to say anything to my father despite the fact that the practice of women taking same-sex mates was common in Dunya. I knew he wanted me to mate with a male and produce heirs. He'd seen me as useless because I was a female, and I was sure he'd regretted that in the moments before his beheading.

Being with Ashera meant that I could be the truest form of myself. I didn't need to hide who I was or what I preferred, and I knew that Ashera would never make me do anything with her other mates unless all parties involved would enjoy it. I didn't find any of the others attractive and would certainly prefer that they didn't touch me unless it was agreed upon with Ashera present.

I truly only wanted to touch and be touched by Ashera.

My dragon purred inside me, blasting me with images of Ashera beneath us as the fire roared to life, the light reflecting off her golden skin and emerald eyes as I brought her ever closer to climax. I wanted to touch, taste, and tease her until she begged me to stop. Suddenly, that was all I could think about.

"I sent them away because I was feeling smothered," she replied.

I blinked. *What?*

It took me a moment to realize that I'd said something before getting lost in thoughts of a moaning, naked Ashera. *Focus, Winta.*

"I can leave if you'd prefer," I offered, though no part of me wanted to leave this room.

She smiled at me. The sight was bright enough to have my heart pounding loudly in my ears.

"I'd love it if you stayed." She motioned me toward her, and I found myself obeying without thought. "It's nice to have another woman around. All the testosterone can be a bit much."

I laughed. "I'm sure."

Ashera pushed the chair back from the desk, allowing me to lean my ass against the desk while facing her. Gods, she was stunning. I traced my fingers over her cheek, basking in the heat her body gave off. As a dragon, I loved it hot.

Brushing my hand down her neck, I pulled her toward me for a kiss, unable to resist the urge to taste her any longer. I wanted her naked against me, breathless and panting, but I didn't want to push her. She eagerly leaned into my touch, her lips soft and insistent against mine. I traced the seam of her lips, needing to deepen the kiss. Her mouth parted instantly, and I swallowed her moans as my tongue met hers. Steadily, I slid my hand from her neck down to the swell of her breasts, the urge to tease more of those moans from her taking over. Her breath hitched as I traced her peaked nipple through her leathers. I couldn't wait to taste them too.

I spun us so she was seated on the edge of the desk. I couldn't hold back anymore. I needed to see her and feel her soft skin moving against mine. I wanted her thighs wrapped around my neck. I wanted her to scream my name. I kissed along her jaw until I reached the soft spot just below her ear. Another moan broke free from her perfect mouth. I could feel the dampness growing in my own pants, and I knew I'd find her wet and wanting too.

I trailed my fingers up her thighs, catching on the holster strapped there. I pulled back from Ashera, knowing I'd find her lips swollen and pupils blown. I loved seeing her hungry for my touch and needy for me, not her other mates. I pulled her daggers from the holster and lifted them until they were dangling from my fingers. I smirked at her questioning look, placed one on the desk beside her, and notched the tip of the other into the leathers covering her legs, slicing through the fabric quickly. I cut the offending material from her body until her perfect pussy was exposed to me. I'd never fucking get tired of the sight.

Leaning down, I trailed kisses up her glorious body, working to remove the leathers hiding the rest of her from me.

She shuddered under my touch, arching toward me hungrily. "Gods, I need to feel you," my mate purred.

Grabbing the dagger I'd left resting beside her, she returned the favor with single-minded focus with her own dagger, cutting the clothes from my body. I shuddered at the scrape of the blade against my skin. I was glad to be free of the leathers, they'd begun to feel suffocating. She dropped the dagger onto the desk and reached up to cup the nape of my neck before gently tugging me forward. For a split second, I debated fighting her pull, but the desire burning within me was too much to resist. I'd let her take control for now. I leaned down, and our mouths connected in a clash of tongues and teeth. We were both desperate, needing more.

Ashera broke the kiss, her mouth hovering over mine as she spoke. "Winta, if you don't fuck me soon, that dagger will be put to better use. Stop fucking teasing me," she growled.

I chuckled, though the threat did nothing but make me ache for her more. Before I could retaliate, she slipped a hand between us and sought out my clit, rubbing slow circles over my swollen bud. It was exquisite, but it wasn't enough. Following her lead, I rested my hands on her hips and stepped back from her teasing fingers before she could get me too close. Her idle threat had given me ideas. I wanted to make her come at least once before I succumbed to her ministrations.

Picking up the dagger, I lowered to my knees before her. My mate. My queen. She watched me closely, her gaze on mine. Both of us were helpless against the need coursing through us. I flipped the weapon in my hand so my palm was wrapped around the blade and kissed my way up the inside of her thigh. Her hands were tangled in my hair, urging me closer to where she wanted me. Reaching her perfect cunt, I breathed in the desire dripping from her. My mouth watered. I licked the arousal coating her thighs before sucking her clit into my mouth. This was what I'd wanted, what I'd needed from my mate. Her hips lifted from the desk, and I slipped my hand between us. I circled her entrance, coating it with the proof of her desire for me. I slipped my finger into her, feeling her walls tighten around it, and cursed at how tight she was, my own desire wetting my thighs. I returned my focus to licking and nipping her clit, slowly pumping my finger into her.

"Gods, yes!" Ashera exclaimed. I could feel her dripping down the palm of my hand. Twisting her fingers through my hair, she began to move against me. I knew that if I kept up the steady strum of my tongue against her swollen bud, she'd break for me soon. I glanced at the dagger in my hand, and a devilish thought entered my mind. I pressed a second finger into her, preparing her for what was to come. I slid my thighs together as my pussy throbbed. I ached to find relief, but Ashera had to come first. My need to see her shatter was stronger than my desire to come.

I knew she was close when her thighs pressed against me, trapping me between her legs. I'd wear them like my favorite necklace forever if I could. She came with my name on her tongue as I savored her release, groaning against her as I tipped closer to the edge. I didn't allow her a second to recover. With my free hand, I slid my fingers from her. Immediately, I replaced them with the hilt. Her eyes flew open in surprise, her gaze slightly unfocused from the orgasm I'd just given her.

She reached for me and tugged me up to stand. I rose slowly, careful not to nick myself on the blade, and straddled her thigh. She trailed her hands over my body like she needed to map out every inch of me before she lost patience and tugged me closer so we were pressed together. The move made the dagger slip deeper inside her, and her moan shot straight to my clit. She was flushed, her breathing was uneven, and her gaze was focused on me as I ground myself against her silky smooth thigh. Moans escaped me at the feel of my wetness spreading on her velvet skin. I was so close already, but I knew I'd need more in order to come. Ashera, sensing my impatience, shoved two fingers inside me, grinning when I gasped at the intrusion.

Her thumb circled my clit as she fucked me with her fingers. I leaned over her farther so she could tease my nipple with her tongue. Any sense of control I had left snapped as I felt my release barreling closer. I fucked her with the hilt of the dagger, the blade digging into the skin of my palm. It could have sliced my hand open, and I doubt I'd have noticed as she crooked her fingers inside of me in a way that made my legs shake.

"I need to taste you," my mate said as I fucked her. She flipped us, surprising me with her strength, tugged me onto the desk with her, and pinned me under her body. Shoving me back onto the cold wood with my legs hanging over the edge, Ashera rested her elbows on either side of my hips. She grasped my knees and spread my legs. An appreciative hum left her as she gazed at my pussy, seeing the proof of my arousal coating me. She then positioned us so her pussy was hovering over my face while her face hovered over mine.

I took in the sight of her dripping cunt and lifted my head off of the desk. With slow, languid strokes, I traced her opening with my tongue. Her hips bucked into me as her lips latched onto my clit. I thrust my tongue into her, wanting to taste her, and her moan vibrated through me. I raised my hips off the desk and pressed myself as close to her mouth as possible. Fuck, her mouth was sinful. I did my best to focus on making sure that I satisfied Ashera as much as she was pleasing me. I sucked her clit into my mouth, swirling my tongue against her while pressing my thumb to her entrance, keeping the dagger in my free hand. I needed to feel her clench around me once more.

I wrapped my arm around Ashera's hips, keeping the dagger pointed away from Ashera, urging her to ride my face as she teased me with her fingers, my come coating her digits as she slowly inserted two of them into me. I burned for her, her breathy moans driving me insane. I bucked against her as she crooked her fingers inside me, finding that perfect spot deep within my channel. Gods, it felt good, but I still craved more. With her, I doubted I'd ever stop wanting more. Ashera's hips bucked as I sucked harder on her clit, groaning as she began to move her hand faster.

I'd never experienced anything more perfect. Tension coiled tighter and tighter inside me as she fucked me with her tongue and her fingers before scraping her teeth across my sensitive flesh. The second she took my clit between her teeth, I cried out against her, my release dragging me under in heavy waves. She came seconds later, and I lapped up every fucking drop she gave me, riding out my orgasm with her. The scrape of metal against wood caught my attention, breaking through the fog of lust in my mind. Ashera lifted her hips, and I immediately lamented the loss, even as curiosity filled me. I adjusted myself, sliding farther beneath her as she dragged cold metal against the sensitive skin on my inner thigh.

Gods, this queen was everything to me. The blunt end of the dagger's hilt pressed against my pussy, and Ashera's moan of appreciation as she watched it slide into me sent heat surging through my veins. Before I got swept up in what she was doing to me, I gripped the blade of my dagger and reached for her, dragging the hilt against her cunt and coating it with her come so it slid inside her with ease. "Have you fed yet, my queen?" I asked as I watched the hilt of the dagger slip in and out of her folds.

"Not yet," she whispered, too entranced to focus on the words leaving her lips.

"Feed, mate, you need it," I insisted as I pushed past the ripples of pleasure racking my body. I knew she'd need it after we were finished. There was no way either of us were walking out of here with an ounce of energy otherwise.

Removing the dagger from deep within me, Ashera flipped it in her grip while moving herself onto the palms of her hands. Gently pressing the blade against the delicate skin of my hip, she glanced back at me, seeking approval. Nodding, I fucked her harder with the hilt of the dagger, anticipating the bite of the blade as she quickly sliced a small cut along my hip bone.

She traced the line of blood now weeping from my skin with her tongue. My hips bucked at the slight sting I felt as she fed, but a fresh flood of arousal left me, and the pain spurred me on. Scenting my need, Ashera pushed the hilt of the dagger toward my entrance and began to fuck me with it once more. Looking between us, I could see blood coating the tip of the blade thrusting between my thighs. My cunt clenched around the hilt. I was so close to coming. Just a few strokes more, I'd be floating through the kind of pleasure only my mate could give me. "Fuck, Ashera, I need to come. I'm so close," I begged as I plunged the dagger into her faster.

Ashera wrapped her luscious lips around the cut and sucked. I could feel my blood sweeping across my hip with Ashera's movements, and my pussy clenched around the dagger. Doing my best not to move too much for fear of cutting her with the blade in my hand, I froze as wave after wave of pleasure surged through me. Sparks burst behind my eyes as Ashera quickened her pace, relentlessly drawing out my orgasm. Ashera followed me over the edge soon after, all the while riding the hilt of the dagger I held.

Panting, Ashera rested her chest against me while slowly pulling the dagger from between my thighs. I heard the clang of it hitting the floor as she released it and began to stroke her hand up and down my leg with featherlight touches. I removed the dagger from her body and licked the come dripping down her thighs, careful not to overstimulate her sensitive flesh.

"Come to bed," she pleaded.

I couldn't deny her.

After a few more moments of basking in each other's presence, we gathered ourselves enough to head naked into her room. It was empty, so we moved to the bathroom where we cleaned each other. We pulled on large shirts and crawled under the sheets together.

The last thought that entered my mind before sleep claimed me was that my precious mate was perfect.

7

ASHERA

There was no way to be sure if Jacobi and Caspian flew to Juniya or not. No means of travel were truly safe right now, but there was merit behind getting to Mazraea quickly. Less exposure meant fewer chances to be attacked on the road. I prayed to any and every god that would listen to keep them safe. I didn't feel any pain or extreme emotions down the bond, which was good if a little unnerving.

I still needed to talk to Malachi and Winta about Judah, though I wasn't sure if there was anything to say. They hadn't come to me yesterday proclaiming victory, so I had to assume he was being a stubborn asshole—what a surprise, a stubborn male asshole in my life. It felt as though the gods, while on my side, wanted to make sure I dealt with every annoying bastard in Dunya. It was rude, if you asked me.

Slipping from bed—not an easy feat with all my mates, except poor Thorne, crammed in with me—I wrapped my cloak around my body and made my way down to the back gardens. I spied them the other day through a window and wanted to take a closer look. It was rare for me to have any time to myself, and I wanted to take this minute to absorb the quiet before the storm.

The gods knew a storm was coming. I sighed as I collapsed to my knees by the fountain, dipping my fingers in the water. We needed to rework our plan now that Judah was here and not in Sahira. We could still utilize the spies we had in Sahira and the surrounding kingdoms to pinpoint Tomas's location. Perhaps it would be prudent to send Malachi to Shaytan, have him ready our army, and begin the march to Masas to meet Qamar's army.

Or was that too much of a threat to Sahira and Juniya?

I ran my hand through my hair in frustration, an annoyed groan making its way past my lips. Objectively, I knew I wasn't alone in making these decisions. I had all of my mates to discuss this with. I liked having a solution or possible solution to an issue to discuss whenever I brought up an issue. I was also the one that had gotten everyone into this disaster in the first place, so shouldn't I also be the one to solve any potential issues that arise?

But here, with this, I felt as though any potential solution I came up with ended in more problems to solve. It wasn't a feeling that sat well with me. It left me feeling like I needed to *do* something instead of sitting here thinking. My limbs tingled with the urge to get up and hack at something, and a jittery sensation coursed its way through my veins.

"You look like you have far too much on your mind, little mate." Thorne's voice startled me out of my depressing thoughts.

I turned to study him. "As I'm sure you're learning, there's quite a bit of work that comes with ruling a kingdom." He was dressed in loose fitting gray linen trousers that hung low on his hips, giving me a glimpse of that delicious V-shape all of my male mates had that drove me wild.

"Especially when one is mated to other rulers from different kingdoms," Thorne replied as he crouched next to me.

His gorgeous chocolate brown eyes were intense as he studied me. I fought the urge to straighten my spine. It was okay for my mate— regardless of whether we'd finalized the bond yet or not—to see me in a moment of weakness. I wanted each of my mates to see every side of me and love everything about me just as I loved everything about them.

"We can't lose, little mate." Thorne gently brushed my hair behind my ear before cupping my cheek. He was so damn warm, and I wanted to melt against him. "If we were on the wrong side of fate, we would not have been matched together, you would not have a mate from almost every kingdom in Dunya, and two stunning queens would never have been able to find themselves seated on their thrones."

I shot him a small smile, grateful that he cared enough to try to cheer me up. It did help to know that my mates were on my side, and I could admit that I hadn't really thought of the fate aspect of all this. Could it be possible that the gods wanted this? That they'd somehow determined long ago that I would be the one to set an apocalyptic change in motion?

A flash of something metallic forced my attention back to Thorne. He had a sword in his hand. Where the hell had he gotten that? I raised my gaze to his in question.

"Why don't we let off some steam?" He grinned down at me. "I'm not stupid enough to test my luck getting between those lush thighs of yours just yet, but a nice sparring match should do the trick."

"You're on, kitten." I lunged to my feet, quick to avoid a swipe of his hand.

"So you want to play dirty, little mate?" He lunged.

I didn't have my daggers on—rookie mistake—which meant I needed to either take the sword from Thorne or disarm him entirely. While I certainly would have preferred getting hold of the blade myself, I'd take either option right now. He was fast and had a suppleness to his movements that left me simultaneously awed and scrambling to get out of reach. It had to be the feline in him. Cats moved in weird ways, and it was always hard to tell if they were a solid or a liquid at any given time.

I had never had any reason to spar with a shifter before, and it quickly became clear that I needed to spar with all of my mates. I was good, but considering we were about to engage in a war that could pit all the species against one another, I needed to make sure I knew how to fight them all. When I wasn't full to bursting from my mates' ever attentive efforts to ensure my magical stores didn't deplete, I could drain opponents without touching them, something no other demon could do, but I couldn't rely on that. My mates kept me far too well fed for that to work on a large group. I'd only been able to feed off Judah the other day because it was just him, and I didn't feed for long. If I starved myself, I'd be able to drain an entire army dry, but there was no way my mates would allow me to do that.

Thorne's hand closed around my neck, violently jerking my thoughts to the present. He swept my legs out from under me, pressing my back against the ground with his body atop mine. I'd be irritated that he managed to best me, but the feel of him had my mind struggling to find anything to complain about. Gods, the man was hard all over. It made my mouth water.

Running his nose along my neck as he took a deep inhale, he murmured, "I can smell how much you need my cock, *kitten.*"

My breath hitched, and my hips arched against his without my permission. He was right, I did need him.

"But naughty kittens don't get cock, do they?" he taunted as he ground against me. "Especially naughty kittens who still haven't put their rabid bloodsucker to task."

He nipped my neck and then stood, backing away from me as I gained my feet. I wanted to punch the goading grin from his face. It shouldn't be as attractive as it was.

"Get your head in the game, kitten." Thorne started to circle me. "I know you fight better than this. Show me."

This was the general of the shifter army. This was the male who helped lead a successful coup. His eyes hardened as he continued to stalk me. I'd trained with Malachi and knew full well he was sizing me up. I wasn't sure if he found me lacking.

I shifted my stance, knowing I needed to get my head out of my ass and focus on not letting him get me on the ground again. I shook my head and closed my eyes, allowing my other senses to take over. He still had that damn sword. That was the first thing that needed to go.

Keeping my eyes closed, I leaned into the air as it dispersed with each movement he made, using that to anticipate where he'd step next. I lost myself to the sensation of moving with the wind as it caressed my body.

"Holy fuck, kitten." The awe in Thorne's voice had me blinking my eyes open.

I had his sword in my hand, the blade held against his neck, and our bodies were pressed together as I pinned him against a tree. My eyes widened in shock. I hadn't even realized I'd disarmed him.

"Well, shit, I knew there was a reason you were the leader and not Malachi, but watching you move is sexy as hell." He dropped his hands to my hips and a purr rumbled his chest.

"I... I've never done anything like that before," I stated.

He nudged the blade of the sword away from his neck with one hand, the other staying firmly planted on my hip. His gaze moved intently over my face, and I fought the urge to squirm.

"Alright. Let's talk about it." Thorne removed the sword from my grip then settled his hand against my hip again, securing me against his rock-hard body.

"I just gave myself over to the feeling of the air around me. I let it guide me." I shrugged and looked past his shoulder to avoid his gaze. The changes my powers had been going through unsettled me a bit, and now was a prime example of that.

"That's not uncommon for an elemental magic user." It wasn't lost on me that he didn't say it wasn't uncommon for a *fae*. "Especially one that has a strong affinity for air. Hell, I've even known water affinities to do the same damn thing around water."

I glanced up at him. "I'm a succubus, Thorne."

"I've noticed." He chuckled.

I rolled my eyes. "I know we haven't really talked about the changes I've been going through lately, but I've never heard of another being able to harness the powers of *all* the species in Dunya. Have you?"

"The only beings I can think of are the gods, but it's questionable whether or not they are even real." Thorne rested his forehead against mine. "Unless these powers are hurting you, you should learn how to use them. We'll need them to win this war."

I nodded. He was right. It wasn't an argument I hadn't heard previously. My other mates had made the same comments before we'd made it to Qamar. I needed to learn to trust them as well as myself.

Thorne bumped his nose against mine. "Kitten, I won't let anything hurt you, not even your powers. I promise."

His lips met mine as my arms wound around his neck. I was surprised by how soft they were. My tongue snaked out just as his did, and we battled for dominance. The purr that had started in his chest picked up again, louder this time. It rumbled through my chest, causing my nipples to tighten.

I tangled my fingers in Thorne's hair as we pressed tighter together. He was all I could feel, smell, and think of. The urge to rip off his clothes and fuck him senseless was almost too much to stand.

Unfortunately, he'd made a good point earlier. I did need to talk to Ambrose. He needed to come to terms with the fact that Thorne was also my mate. Soon.

Thorne pulled away after nipping my lower lip. "I'm going to bring you back into the house, kitten. I won't take you without your other mates being well aware of what's happening."

~

Jacobi

ASHERA, *my love, my mate, shone in the moonlight. Her golden skin seemed to glitter as she turned to me. We were somehow back in my old rooms at the palace in Shaytan. Gods, she was the most stunning thing I'd ever seen in all my seven hundred plus years. I didn't think I could ever get enough of simply looking at her.*

I'd never known I could want something as much as I wanted her. I'd never thought myself a possessive male, but gods, when it came to my lovely mate... unless it was one of her other mates, I would never let another touch her. I would happily kill for her. I would absolutely die for her. I would give up my kingdom for her. Anything she asked of me.

And yet, I knew she would never ask me to do any of those things. She didn't expect us to go to war with her. If I'd voiced any hesitation, she would have understood and would not have asked me to compromise my standing in any way. The only thing she wanted from any of her mates was their love and affection. Two things that were so easy to give her.

"Jacobi." Ashera's voice was smooth as sin, just as it always was. "My angel king."

She came to me, arms raised, and pressed her hands against my chest. The feel of her against me...gods, there was nothing better. Her skin, so soft and supple, felt warm against mine, causing a carnal hunger to stir deep within me.

I needed to taste her. If I didn't, I was sure I would die.

My lips claimed hers in a bruising kiss; I wasn't able to hold myself back from the siren song that was Ashera. Everything about her called to me on a primal level. I needed to claim her. Here. Now.

As though my thoughts were magic, Ashera and I were suddenly naked and pressed tightly together. Her scent perfumed the air around us with her arousal, and it spurred me on. My need turned frantic as her small, delicate hand wrapped around my rigid cock.

I ripped my lips from hers, my gaze scanning the room around us. The bed was too far away, but there was a small table mere steps behind my gorgeous mate. Growling low in my throat, I scooped her up and gently laid her on the table. My own personal feast.

I planned to gorge myself on her.

Dropping to my knees, I allowed my gaze to travel over her before our eyes locked. Heat flared in her emerald depths, and my breath caught. I loved that look. Loved the heat.

"You're going to want to hold on to something, my love." That was the only warning she got before I lowered my mouth to her clit.

Her small gasping exhale was quickly followed by her frantic fingers tangling themselves in my hair. My mouth continued its assault as I slid two fingers into her pussy, crooking them slightly before rubbing them against the spot I knew drove her wild. It wasn't enough. Would never be enough. I needed to feel her come unraveled. Hear her scream my name to the heavens.

I rarely used my gifts to manipulate other's emotions. It was a violation, and wasn't something I planned on doing now. But my sweet mate was learning how to use a similar power, so I opened myself to her. I allowed her to feel my pleasure as I feasted on her, allowed her to feel how good her slick pussy felt pulsing around my fingers, how hard I was, how desperate I was to feel her milking my cock.

"Jacobi!" Ashera cried as her hips arched off the table.

She soon became incoherent, her head flung back in the throws of passion, hands tugging on my head, and legs squeezing around my face. But it still wasn't enough.

I flooded her with my love next. That burning passion I felt only for her and the tenderness she inspired in me. I gave myself over to her and left myself an open book.

"Gods! Yes!" Her cry was music to my ears.

But it still wasn't enough.

Using magic, I created several hands that ran down her body, played with her nipples, and teased her as my tongue circled and swiped at her clit. My fingers remained buried inside her, pulsing against her g-spot. Finally, using my other hand, which had been anchored to the outside of her thigh, I eased a finger into her tight ass.

I could feel her about to topple over the edge into oblivion, so I eased back, biting back a smirk when she cursed me out.

"Come now, my love," I soothed, making sure my lips brushed against her clit as I spoke. "Good things come to those who wait."

"Don't tease me," Ashera moaned. "Please."

"Gods above, I love when you start to beg," I growled. "You're not begging nearly enough for you to come. But you will."

Her whimper quickly turned into a pleasured moan as I went back to teasing every inch of her. My mouth left her clit only when my fingers could take over. I brought her to the edge over and over again, losing all sense of time as I kept her from coming.

Until finally, "Please! Jacobi!" she cried. "Please! Gods, I need you so bad."

Our skin glistened with sweat as I rose above her, my wicked grin causing her to let out a small whimper.

"You begged like such a good girl," I praised. "Would you like your reward?"

"Gods, yes," she begged.

Gripping her thighs in both hands, I spread her wide for me. I took a moment to enjoy her flushed face and chest, her body dripping with sweat as her chest heaved in and out. But the sight that I loved most of all was her drenched pussy fully on display. My cock hardened even more as I started to ease myself into her.

Fuck. Watching her take every damn inch of me created a feeling almost impossible to describe. I felt like a god.

"Take all of me, my love," I groaned as I continued to push into her. "That's it."

Her hips tilted as I bottomed out. "Such a good girl," I said through gritted teeth. "So tight and fucking wet for me."

"Move," she pleaded.

I moved her legs to my shoulders, and put a leg up on the table before pressing our chests closer together, letting out a vicious snarl at how she damn near strangled my cock at this angle. I braced one hand on her hip, and the other came up to wrap around her slender throat.

"I'm going to fuck this pussy until you're dripping with my come, my love. I'm going to use it as I see fit. Now squeeze my cock tighter and moan for me."

My first thrust was hard. I wasn't the pure, chaste angel king anymore. I was this amazing queen's mate. She'd unleashed something primal and savage in me that first night. Something that hungered for her above everything else. Something that would never be satisfied. Something that would tear the world apart just to be buried in her hot depths over and over again.

I'd tried to keep it contained. No more. I wanted to savage her. I wanted to own her.

Each snap of my hips against her caused her gorgeous tits to bounce and her eyes to flutter. My hand around her throat kept her anchored in place. All too soon, my lovely mate was screaming my name, chanting it like a prayer, her pussy fluttering wildly around my cock. I adjusted my angle so my hips hit against her clit with each thrust.

Ashera turned wild beneath me. Her hands gripped my biceps, nails digging into the skin there. I just tightened my grip around her throat and fucked her harder, faster.

"You're going to come all over my cock," I demanded. "Do it now, love."

Gods, I'd never felt anything as amazing as Ashera squeezing the life out of my dick.

I came with a roar as her scream filled the air.

"I don't want to judge you," Caspian's voice coupled with the explosive orgasm I'd just experienced, jolted me awake, "but coming in your sleep like that..."

"Fuck off," I grumbled.

Ashera

WE WERE GATHERED around Thorne's kitchen table. It seemed that was our go-to meeting spot now. To be honest, things felt off without Caspian and Jacobi. I missed them far more than I thought I would. Caspian's hotheadedness kept us all on our toes, and Jacobi's calming nature made sure that nothing ever got out of hand.

"We weren't able to get anything concrete out of Judah," Malachi began. "And not without some lying and physical persuasion on our end."

Ambrose growled. Thorne groaned. I ran my hand through my hair.

"So how do we want to handle that?" I asked.

"I think it's safe to say that we shouldn't trust him," Winta replied. "No matter what he says, if he was really on our side, he would have said something to us before our interrogation turned physical."

"So he's in league with Tomas? Do we use that? *Can* we use that?" I looked to Ambrose.

"My father doesn't give a shit about anyone other than himself," Ambrose snarled. "He doesn't give a fuck if Judah dies. In fact, I wouldn't be surprised if the asshole wasn't rubbing his hands together in glee right now. He's in the perfect position to step in as ruler of Sahira, at least until he can find another witch he can manipulate to take the throne."

"Then do we let Judah go and have spies follow him in the hopes he leads us to Tomas?" I questioned as I glanced around.

"It's either that or see if he wants to dig himself a hole by trying to get close to us," Malachi replied with a shrug.

"Why don't we see what he says? Make it seem as though we're attempting to be reasonable with him?" Winta suggested.

I nodded. "Okay. We need to make sure that we have someone watching him closely."

"Don't worry, little queen," Ambrose growled with a vicious smirk. "That asshole won't go anywhere without one of us hearing about it."

"It's looking more and more like we're heading for a large battle," Thorne eventually commented. "I'm more than happy to have men go to Masas to help Ambrose take the throne there, but I don't want to leave Qamar unprotected."

"I agree," Malachi said. "I was thinking about going to get a small unit of highly trained men from Shaytan, mobilizing the army while I'm there, before heading down to Masas to help. I can fly no problem, so it shouldn't take me long. All of the men I have in mind can fly too, which means we can make it to Masas in record time."

My heart lurched at the thought of being separated from yet another mate. It made sense, and it wouldn't be for long.

"That's a solid plan." Thorne nodded before continuing, "I know the original plan was for Ambrose and me to go to Masas together, but I think it's best if we travel together now that Judah showed his ugly face."

Everyone nodded.

"I'll head out to Shaytan now," Malachi said as he stood. "Since I need to go north as you all travel south, I expect us to be about a day or so behind you."

"It'll take me about a day to get everything ready here," Thorne responded. "So that timing should work perfectly."

I stood and made my way over to Malachi, pulling him out of the room as the other three started talking about travel plans. I didn't need to pay too much attention to that.

"Please be safe," I murmured, digging my nails into Mal's arm.

"Sher, there is nothing on this earth that could keep me away from you." He wrapped his arms around me and pressed his forehead against mine. "You are my very soul. I promise that I will always find you. Always."

My eyes slid closed as I basked in his body heat. Malachi had always been my rock, which made parting with him harder than any of the others.

As if sensing my struggle, Mal gripped my chin and tilted my face up to his. I opened my eyes, and I became trapped in his stunning honeyed gaze.

"I will do whatever it takes to keep you safe, Sher. *Whatever it takes.*" His voice was a harsh rumble that had my heart stuttering in my chest. "I never hoped for anything like you, and the gods still placed you in my care. I will forever be grateful and humbled that you are my mate. I will light this entire world on fire before I let you go. I spent too long denying what was between us. Now, I'd sacrifice everyone and everything just to keep what we have. You. Are. *Everything.*"

A tear slid down my cheek as our lips met. This male. Gods, he killed me. There were days when I wasn't sure I deserved him, but even on those days, I was selfish enough to cling to him like a lifeline. I would destroy the world for Malachi.

Mal pulled away, and we stared at one another for a long moment.

"I'm coming back to you, Sher." With that, he pressed a brief kiss against my forehead and strode off.

After making my way back into the kitchen with the others, Ambrose slid his chair closer to mine and wrapped his arm around me. I gave him a small smile, thankful for the bit of comfort he offered without bitching.

"We're going to go see what Judah has decided to do," Winta informed me. "I'm going to take Thorne up with me. Do you want to stand outside the door?"

A thought struck me. "Actually," I said with a grin, "I want to go in the room... alone."

Everyone stiffened. Before they could say anything, I held up a hand. "Hear me out. We know, either way, that he is most likely going to betray us. His sense of urgency will be greater if he knows I'm alive."

"Which means he's more likely to fuck up sooner," Thorne concluded.

"Exactly," I replied with a grin. "The resistance is going to know I'm alive once we get to Masas anyway. There's no way we can take that entire kingdom without a fight, and I'll probably be seen." I shot each of them a glare. "There is no way I would sit out during a fight like that, so there's no point in trying to talk me out of it."

"I didn't want to think about it," Ambrose confessed. "But you're right."

"The others aren't going to like it," Winta pointed out.

"I won't sit aside while the rest of you risk your lives like that. I'm hiding from the resistance in the hopes that they will show us where Tomas is, but this is our best shot at finding him! Judah is going to lead us right to him, and he isn't even going to realize it. If he claims he wants to help, act as though you believe him and say that you have something to tell him in good faith, and then I'll walk into the room."

"And if he doesn't want to help?" Thorne asked.

"Then I'll walk in to show him that his friends all failed." I shrugged.

Ambrose rubbed his temples. "Little queen, you're going to give me an aneurysm."

"Not if this works."

"If, she says!" Ambrose growled. "If!"

Winta studied me silently from across the table before nodding. "I'm with Ashera."

Thorne and Ambrose groaned and placed their heads on the table.

"Of course they side with each other!" Thorne's voice was muffled as he spoke against the wooden surface.

"It's easier if we just give in to what she wants," Ambrose grumbled.

AN HOUR LATER, I found myself standing outside the door to Judah's room. Winta had made a very specific and bold move by placing him here. He was a guest, and he was royalty, but that clearly didn't count for much with her. She wouldn't treat him like a common prisoner, but there was no royal fanfare to be seen.

It was a very nice political snub. I loved it.

"You're saying you'll help?" I could hear the disbelief in Winta's voice through the closed door. "Why?"

"I'm not claiming I'm doing this for pure purposes," Judah responded. "I'd just rather be on the winning side of this fight."

Fair enough, I supposed. Once a coward, always a coward.

"I don't have an heir," Judah continued. "So if I die, someone far worse may take power in Sahira. Do you want that to happen?"

No. No, we do not want that to happen.

"Point taken," Thorne said.

"In that case" —Winta's voice sounded closer to the door— "we have something we'd like to show you. As a gesture of goodwill."

The door creaked open, and I stepped into the room. Judah's sharp intake of breath and wide eyes said that I was the last person he thought would cross the threshold. Good. The resistance really thought I was dead.

"Ashera," he murmured, his eyes glued to me.

"King Judah." I tilted my head as I studied him. "I hear you want to help."

I allowed my empathic abilities to flood the room as I attempted to gauge every little reaction he made. The overwhelming feeling I was getting from him was shock, but the others were too muddled to make out. I really needed Jacobi to teach me how to read emotions better when we were reunited.

"I can't say that I'm pleased to see you," Judah remarked as he stood from his position on the bed. "While I hadn't ordered my people to attack you in Masas, I hadn't exactly been torn up about your death either."

"At least you're being honest," I replied. At least I thought he was being honest. It was still hard to tell. "I figured I'd show myself if you decided to work with my mates to prove that we wouldn't just cut your head off whenever we felt like it."

He laughed. "You still might." His eyes narrowed. "Mates?" He glanced at Thorne and Winta.

"Malachi, Ambrose, Caspian, and Jacobi," I said. I didn't want to feed the resistance more information about my other mates if they didn't already know. "I know you know about them and their alliance with Qamar."

Judah studied the three of us, suspicion shining bright in his gaze before he nodded. "Yes, I know all about that. It's why I came here."

I crossed my arms over my chest. "Is it really? I doubt that. If Tomas ran off to Sahira after Qamar fell, you either came here to test Winta's and Thorne's strength, form a secret alliance of your own, or attempt to start another coup against the new rulers."

"You're smarter than you look." Gods, I wanted to punch the condescension right out of him. "I'm still not convinced you didn't fuck your way to the head of your coup, but that comment alone suggests you aren't just a pretty little simpleton."

I placed my hand against my chest in mock flattery. "Did you two hear that?" I asked excitedly. "He doesn't think I'm a pretty little simpleton!"

My gaze hardened as I took a step toward Judah. I relaxed my grip on all of my powers just enough for him to feel a small amount of the power I wielded. His eyes grew even wider than they had when I'd entered the room, and he took a step to the side and back so he could press his spine against the wall.

"Coward," I sneered.

8

AMBROSE

We made our way through Qamar with a not so small army trudging ahead of us. Ashera and I had opted to stay at the rear to keep curious gazes away from my little queen. Thorne had suggested a route along Malak and Qamar's shared border. We didn't want to cross into Malak without the king with us to prevent any unnecessary political faux pa. It would take a lot longer than a day or two at the rate we were marching to reach Masas. We still needed to cross the damn mountains.

Thankfully, the road we traveled on was flat with fields on either side. The people of Qamar raised livestock throughout their kingdom, and this must be one of their herd's grazing areas. Though, I was sure the entire kingdom was one large grazing field. Still, it was vastly different from the rocky and mountainous terrain that made up Masas. My home kingdom was harsh, even for those of us born there. Compared to Masas, Qamar seemed...soft.

Walking with such a large number of soldiers would take time, which meant that Malachi, unless he flew over us on his way to Masas, would get there a lot faster than we would. He'd know that this route was the best for any number of soldiers headed south, so I hoped he would fly along this route to search for us with his demon buddies.

Ashera had filled me in on what had happened yesterday with Judah, and I wanted to rip that fucker's throat out for suggesting that my little queen was an idiot. I realized how hypocritical I sounded, as I'd assumed the same thing before meeting her. But I knew the truth now. Ashera was brilliant. She doubted herself, even when she shouldn't, but her instincts were usually spot on, and she had a killer wit. One that intimidated the shit out of most males.

Thankfully, I wasn't most males. Well...not anymore. I found everything about my little queen amazing and arousing.

"Ambrose?" Ashera's voice pulled my gaze from where it had been locked on the soon-to-be dead witch king, down to her as she walked at my side. "Where did your mind wander off to?"

"Murder and mayhem," I replied with a smirk that had her rolling her eyes.

"It's always either killing or sex with you." She laughed as she bumped her shoulder against me.

"You're telling me there's more to life than bleeding people dry and fucking your tight little pussy?" I made sure to lace my tone with shock. "Since fucking when?"

Ashera's laugh was musical and lit up my spirit better than anything else ever could. I grinned down at her as she shook her head. It had been a while since we'd been able to just joke around with one another. It was good to hear her laugh. Hopefully soon, she'd be able to do it more often.

"Tell me the thought of me letting that witch fucker bleed to death and then fucking you in his blood doesn't appeal to you," I challenged.

"I try not to lie to you," she responded, causing me to burst out laughing.

That was yet another thing I loved about my little queen; I never knew what the fuck was going to come out of her mouth at any given minute. Gods, she was perfect.

"As cute as this moment is," a vaguely familiar voice said from behind us, "it's really not what you should be focused on."

We both spun to face the stranger we'd encountered in the forest on our way to Qamar. He was an odd looking fucker. I'd never seen someone who had features from every species in Dunya before. He was

tall like the shifters, with feral looking eyes that matched theirs—
suggesting he potentially had an animal form—pointed ears like the
fae, fangs that peaked out of his smirk, demon horns, and gray angelic
wings.

I stepped in front of Ashera with a snarl. "Who the fuck are you?"

I could feel Ashera lean against me as she rose on her tip-toes to
get a better look. I fought the urge to slap my hand against her eyes. I
didn't want her looking at this fucker. My growl grew louder.

"Easy." The stranger chuckled. "I'm just here to check in on my
goddess."

I'm sorry...Did he just say his *goddess?*

Ashera's hands gripped onto my arms, keeping me in place. I
wanted to lunch at him and rip him limb from fucking limb. Ashera
was not his goddess.

"He's so easily riled," the stranger pointed out, addressing Ashera
directly. "Do you all taunt him for fun?"

I could feel Ashera's body shaking slightly behind me. Rationally, I
knew better than to interpret that as fear, but my brain was so far gone
that fear was the only thing it could come up with. Which only pissed
me off more.

"Listen, asshole— "I started with a snarl.

"Daimon," asshole cut me off. "The name is Daimon."

"Ambrose," Ashera's sweet voice broke through my rage haze as
she stepped around me, placing me behind her. "Take a few deep
breaths."

"I'd listen to her, she can fuck you up," Daimon pointed out with a
taunting smirk.

"Don't, Ambrose," Ashera warned. "Don't let him get to you."

"Fine," I grumbled. "But on your say-so, I get to kill him."

"Okay," she soothed.

"She's not going to want to kill me," Daimon said with a laugh.

"And why is that, exactly?" Ashera asked as she crossed her arms
over her chest and popped out her hip.

"I can't tell you everything, goddess!"

I swear, if that fucker called her goddess one more fucking time...

"Ashera! Ambrose! Do you want to be left behind?" We both turned at the sound of Thorne's shout. When we turned back, Daimon was gone.

"What the actual fuck was that?!" I yelled, glancing around to try to spot the asshole.

"I have no idea." Ashera sighed but nudged me into walking alongside her once again. "But we need to catch up."

~

Ashera

HOURS HAD PASSED since we'd set out on our trek. We'd made progress, but not enough to stifle the irritation that had been building deep inside me. I had done my best to keep my expression stoic, and the earlier conversation with Ambrose had helped to lift my spirits some.

Too many thoughts still clouded my mind. I worried about Jacobi and Caspian, wondering if things were going smoothly for them. I thought about the task Malachi now faced, and the fact that we still had at least another day's travel ahead of us. My mind seemingly caught in a never-ending swirl of morose thoughts.

Deciding I needed to distract myself, I studied my surroundings.

There were more cows along the Qamar border than I ever cared to see. It was evident that the farmers here had a love for beef; one that I shared with them. My mouth watered at the mental image of sitting around a fire with my mates and filling myself with some well roasted red meat.

When my gaze drifted from the calves, huddled together in the shade beneath the branches of a large tree, I caught sight of Bradford slightly stumbling over a crack in the path ahead. He fixed his footing before I could reach for him and carried on walking. Before now, I hadn't paid much attention to him with everything happening to and around us, but from the little time I'd spent with him, he seemed nice.

I reached out with my empathic powers and took stock of how everyone was feeling. Stress seemed to rule the day. Tension rang, and I once more felt guilty for subjecting my mates--as well as these soldiers-

-to the chaos I'd caused. I brushed the feeling aside, forcing myself not to focus on it when I couldn't afford to let my guard down out in the open. I kept focus on the group as a whole. Ambrose and Winta were chatting behind me but I chose not to eavesdrop. My mates needed to learn to co-exist. Ambrose just had to learn to live with Thorne's addition to the group.

Ahead of me, Bradford walked alone, keeping himself company as he watched our surroundings eagerly. I was curious about him. We'd spent a couple of short moments in each other's company, but I'd never been given the chance to learn much about him. I took a step forward, determined to seize this opportunity and strike up a conversation. Just as I was about to reach Bradford, he tripped again, his large body crashing downward. Reaching out, I caught his elbow and stopped him from eating dirt.

Startled by my touch, he steadied himself then immediately backed away from my hand. His cheeks darkened with the blush while he averted his green eyes from mine. Lifting his head he checked to make sure my overly possessive vampire wasn't about to rip his arm from his body for touching me. I couldn't stop the chuckle that erupted from me when I noted he'd turned his attention to the sky, the trees, anything but me in an attempt to appear as innocent as possible.

"You know, while I appreciate the effort you're putting into ensuring our safety, I'd love it if you could do so without face planting the ground. I don't think the other soldiers will cut you a break for the mark you'll be sporting when it inevitably happens," I admonished, allowing a teasing lilt to creep into my tone.

"I... I will do my best your --" he paused, no longer knowing how best to address me. We avoided using my title at all costs when in public, and even in cases like this where we seemed relatively alone. It was best for everyone if the majority of the soldiers here didn't know who I truly was. We wanted to avoid an ambush. We also wanted to ensure that if anything happened, we knew who the leak was.

Daimon cropping up out of nowhere had just further proved to us that no matter how safe we thought we were, no matter how well hidden we believed I could remain, anyone could find us.

"Call me Ash," I said, nodding. I didn't want him to refer to me as

Sher, that was Mal's nickname for me. "I suspect we're going to know each other well enough by the time this mess is over, so we may as well become familiar with each other now," I stated, knowing that if things continued as they had, Bradford would be seeing a lot more of the world than just Qamar and Masas.

We continued walking for a few more moments in silence. I spied Bradford looking at me hesitantly out of the corner of my eye. He seemed unsure of how to start a conversation. I decided to put the gentle giant out of his misery.

"So, Winta mentioned before that you're mated?" I asked, hoping that I hadn't overstepped by asking about his personal life. I stood by the idea of getting to know him though, and thought of no better way to do so than by encouraging him to speak about the things and people he loved.

Facing me, his entire demeanor changed. Gone were the questioning glances, and in their place, a prideful expression seeped across his features. Having left my empathic powers open, I could feel the pride and love explode through him at the mere mention of his mate. I was glad for it. I loved my mates so fiercely, I struggled to imagine being fated to spend an entire lifetime with someone I couldn't stand to be near.

"Yes. Caoimhe is my mate," Bradford proudly exclaimed, a toothy smile breaking free across his naturally serious face. It was evident from that one answer that he held her in high regard. He loved her. My heart warmed at the sight of his smile, and I hoped that thoughts of me brought my mates similar feelings.

"We're expecting our first child together soon," he beamed. Shock flooded my body and I paused at the mention of a child. They were so rare. Many of our kind tried and hoped for children, but so few existed. The majority of pregnancies ended in miscarriage, or the death of the mother, and often the babe.

"Wow, congratulations! How...How far along is she?" I gasped as the words tumbled out of my mouth. I'd never encountered someone that experienced pure joy when speaking about a pregnancy. The few I'd known had felt trepidation at the prospect of losing their mate.

"She's seven months along. We've tried many times in the past, with no luck. Having children together is even harder for interspecies couples. My mate unfortunately miscarried every time, but both Caoimhe and I are certain that this time," he paused, considering his phrasing before finally announcing, "This time the gods are on our side."

It was a strong declaration to make, but I hoped he was right. The affection he felt for the child Caoimhe carried was already tangible. I could feel it sweep through me. It was overwhelming--pure love, joy and devotion to his family. The contrast against my own sorrow and anxiety for them was far too noticeable. I shut my empathic powers down, feeling too vulnerable to balance my own warring emotions with his. I looked away briefly, hoping I'd managed to rearrange my face into something more suitable for his mood. The last thing I wanted to do was ruin the happiness he felt. I couldn't bear to do that to him.

We began walking again and--after gathering myself--I rested my hand against his forearm and breathed a sigh before saying, "Well, regardless of whether the gods are on your side or not, you have us. Me."

"Thank you Ash," he whispered, his voice filled with awe and tenderness. His features softened as he glanced at me before gently patting my hand and curtly nodding his head.

I decided right then and there that I liked Bradford. He was kind, caring and nurturing. He loved his family. He hadn't been corrupted by the nobles of Qamar, and he took his station very seriously. If I could do anything at all to help either he or Caoimhe over the next two months I would do it. I'd missed having a friend, someone outside of my mates to share small moments with, to speak freely with. I was glad for the friendship I now seemed to share with him.

~

LATER THAT NIGHT, Ambrose and I settled in beside the fire some of the shifter soldiers had made when we'd stopped to make camp. My thoughts kept floating back to Daimon. Who the hell was he? We hadn't seen him since we'd first made our way to Qamar. Then, he'd

138 | ELIZABETH BROWN

appeared against a tree to tell my mates and I that I'd never been a slave. He'd even insinuated that I didn't really know what I was.

This time he'd appeared to antagonize Ambrose and...check on me? I felt drawn to him, but was that because he seemed to know things about me? Our interactions were too brief for me to really tell.

It frustrated me. The last thing I needed was another threat to contend with. Especially not with someone who seemed to know more about me than I did. I had to hope Daimon was at least on our side.

"Don't let him get to you," Ambrose murmured against my ear.

I turned, tilting my head up to study him. I was surprised he wasn't pissed. That was Ambrose's usual M.O. Freak out about things and then deal with the fall out. I narrowed my eyes in suspicion.

"What are you planning?" I asked.

"I may have an idea if he shows up again." Ambrose shrugged. "But you're already under a lot of pressure and stress. I don't want you getting stuck in your head."

"Valid point," I sighed.

Footsteps approaching had both of us looking to our left to see Winta, Thorne and Judah making their way over. We'd kept to the back of the group to keep eyes off me, but by now everyone was too damn tired to really care too much about what went on.

"Did everything go okay?" Winta asked as they all took a seat around the fire.

"We had a run in with someone," I said. Ambrose huffed and slid me a glare. "I'm not here to hide shit, Ambrose."

His eyes slid to Judah and then back to me. I understood his worry, but I didn't see the harm in talking about Daimon in front of the witch king. If Daimon was part of the resistance, Judah would know about him, and would hopefully give that away. I also wanted to play along with "trusting" him.

"Did any of the men give you a problem?" Thorne asked, leaning forward with an intense gaze. "Tell me which one it was and I'll personally rip his dick off."

Ambrose groaned dramatically and rolled his eyes. I bit back a laugh.

"None of your men gave us any problems," I said, smiling when

Thorne relaxed. "I believe we told you we'd run into someone we didn't know on the way to Qamar?"

They both nodded.

"We ran into him again," I said with a shrug. "Said his name is Daimon and that he was just checking up on me."

Judah's face didn't change, and I didn't pick up any change in his emotions either. He approached us calmly and remained that way. Which meant he most likely didn't know who Daimon was. I wasn't sure whether to be relieved or disappointed.

"Never heard of him." Thorne looked at Winta who shook her head. "What does he look like?"

Ambrose and I took turns describing the mystery male. I'd never met someone who looked like Daimon...except...maybe...

Ambrose, Thorne, and Winta all stared at me, making me wince. I have a sneaking suspicion I knew what they were thinking, and I wasn't sure I was ready to hear it. *I* looked like Daimon. *I* had the features of several species. *I* had the powers of several species.

Gods, what *was* I?

The others, aside from Judah, cast worried glances at each other before turning their faces carefully neutral. They didn't want to discuss this around Judah, neither did I. There might be a few things I didn't mind the witch king knowing, but this certainly wasn't information I felt comfortable sharing.

"He doesn't sound familiar," Winta finally commented. "Perhaps Thorne should travel with you tomorrow."

"No." I shook my head. "It's fine. I'm not worried about him. Just figured it was something to note."

Winta nodded but threw a glance at Thorne. I had a feeling my mates wouldn't take any chances. Surprise flew through me when Thorne and Ambrose shared a look before nodding. Even those two were teaming up on this? I wanted to be offended, but I knew this stemmed from caring for me and not a lack of faith in my abilities to keep myself safe.

The thundering sound of wings beating against the sky had all of us looking up. That sound could only mean the arrival of one person... Malachi. My heart soared at the thought of seeing my incubus assassin again. He'd certainly made good time if he was meeting us on the way to Masas. Then again, we'd also been held up with all the soldiers we were bringing with us from Qamar.

I glanced over at the others, who were also glancing skyward. All except Judah, who was staring intently at me over the dance of the flames. Malachi had mentioned, after his first interaction with the king, that something felt off about him. I couldn't help but agree. There was something dark in his gaze, almost as though his soul was missing.

I fought back a shiver and returned my gaze to the sky. "Malachi is here," I announced and stood, the others following suit.

"That was quick," Thorne said, sounding impressed. "I'm envious of how fast he can get people to move." He shot a quick glance at the pitched tents and soldiers around us.

"He did say he would only need to gather some of his best men," Winta reminded. "It's easier to move faster with wings and not as many men."

"Trust me," I said with a grin, "he won't need many men with the soldiers he's chosen."

Thorne turned a bloodthirsty smile on me. "Excellent."

~

Malachi

WHEN I'D ARRIVED in Shaytan, I was pleased to find that Tobias, my second in command, had taken it upon himself to mobilize the army upon hearing Ashera had fallen in Masas. He wanted to secure our borders, as well as attempt to weed out any members of the resistance that still called our kingdom home.

Tobias and I had been assassins together for many, many years. We'd trained under the same master and had moved up the ranks in the army together. He'd been the first person I'd approached when Ashera and I had started to cement our plans of a coup.

Tobias's closest lieutenant, Kyra, had also been present when I touched down at the palace. She was an excellent marksman and strategist. The two of them together...well, I was happy they'd been on our side during the coup.

Tobias and Kyra were able to quickly mobilize our most elite unit, and after a brief squabble over which one would come with me to face down the resistance, Tobias was now flying to my right. I had a sneaking suspicion Kyra wasn't about to let this go any time soon. He'd need to watch his back when we made it back to Shaytan.

It had taken mere hours to gather everything we needed before we were airborne. I'd filled Tobias in on everything as we flew, keeping my voice low so the others wouldn't overhear. I trusted them all, but I wasn't about to take any unnecessary risks with Ashera's life if I didn't need to.

"I'll confer with Thorne when we land," Tobias said as we approached the shifter camp. A scout had spotted it about an hour ago and I was relieved to know we would be joining up with Ashera and the others before they reached Masas. "You go see your mate."

"Once you've found yours, you'll understand my rush." I laughed. Tobias was in no hurry to find his mate, ever the ladies man. "She'll knock some serious sense into you, old friend."

He scowled at me and shook his head. "I'll pass. Now get down there before I break your nose."

"That statement suggests you'd be able to land a punch, kid." I swerved out of the way when he rushed me. "You'll have to be faster than that."

"When you least expect it, old man."

We began our descent, my heart racing at the thought of seeing Ashera again. I hurled myself through the air, pulling my wings back so that I could reach her as quickly as possible. I spied her sitting next to the campfire, curled into Ambrose's embrace.

Extending my wings and catching the updraft, I lowered myself gently to the ground just before her. Too impatient to acknowledge anyone else, I wrapped an arm around her waist, the other curving beneath her legs, and hauled her up into my arms, crushing her against my chest.

I needed to feel my mate. To have the warmth of her skin pressed against mine. We'd barely spent a day apart, but my body pulsed with the need to consume her.

Before she could utter a single word I pressed my lips to hers.

The noise from the camp faded into the background as our lips danced, fighting for dominance. Ashera moaned just as my tongue brushed against hers. That single sound was enough to shatter my restraint.

My cock swelled as her body thrummed with need. I could feel her arousal stirring through the bond. I deepened the kiss, nipping and sucking at her bottom lip. She tasted so good, but I craved more.

I wanted to be inside of her. I wanted her writhing beneath me, screaming my name for everyone to fucking hear.

Tightening my hold around her waist, I unfurled my wings and pushed us into the air. Ashera squealed at the shock of suddenly being airborne while wrapping her hands around my neck.

"Mine," I growled, nuzzling my head against her delicate neck.

Beneath us I could hear Ambrose bitching, but I elected to ignore him and flew us higher. Peeking over Ashera's shoulder, I spotted a secluded tree. It had caught my eye during my earlier descent, and I knew that it was the perfect spot to fuck my mate. I needed to remind her who she belonged to.

"Yours, Mal, I'm yours," Ashera whispered as she pressed gentle kisses along my chin.

A few beats later, I was lowering us toward the ground, planting my feet firmly before holding Ashera against the curve of the tree. Her back arched as her legs slipped down and wrapped around my waist.

My dick strained inside of my leathers as she tightened her hold on me. Softly, I pushed my hips against hers before stepping back from between her legs.

"I need to get these leathers off you Sher, I have to feel you," I groaned. Her hands clawed at my shoulders, silently begging me to keep pressure on her pussy.

"Fine," she growled, her voice dripping with desire. Before I could even reach for her cloak, Ashera was half tearing her training leathers from her body.

Soaking in the sight of her creamy flesh, I watched as her breasts swayed with each movement she made. Working as quickly as I could, I undid the ties to my own leathers, letting them fall to the ground before stepping back into Ashera's hold.

Her nipples tightened as she brushed against my chest, the slight touch setting my skin on fire. My cock bobbed along her stomach, the precum already leaking from it spreading across her skin. I could feel myself throbbing at the sight. I loved marking my mate. Loved knowing my scent would be all over her. Loved that when she returned to the others, she wouldn't be able to deny who she'd been with.

I knew the love she felt for me was strong and real. So much so, that she would never think to deny our bond, let alone who had been buried deep inside her. Yet I couldn't ignore the sense of relief I felt anytime I marked her with my scent. I wanted the world to know that she was mine.

Wrapping my hand around Ashera's thighs, I lifted her while firmly pressing her into the tree. I needed to be careful with how much I pushed her so as not to cause her pain, even if my little slut did like it.

Despite the desire coursing through my veins, I wanted to cherish this moment. It was seldom for us to have a minute to ourselves. Just this once I'd be selfish, I'd take my time and keep her for a while longer. At this moment I didn't want to share her, to watch the others feasting on what was mine. I had no desire for them to see pleasure wrack her body, or watch my come leak between her velvet thighs.

Rubbing the tip of my dick against her opening, I relished the feel of the wetness pooling there. "Fuck, Sher, you're dripping," I hissed, my cock slowly pushing inside her. Her pussy fluttered with anticipation, and her thighs wrapped around me like a vice.

"Please, Mal, don't make me beg. I want you," she moaned, her hand grasping the back of my neck as her fingers entwined with my hair.

Unable to resist her anymore, my hips surged forward of their own accord and buried my dick deep in her tight wet cunt.

"Yes," she groaned. "Fuck me Mal, please, I've missed you. I need you to move," Ashera begged as I slowly moved my hips, thrusting myself in and out of her pussy.

I picked up the pace, working to build a steady rhythm. I adjusted my hold, moving one hand to wrap behind her back, while the other snaked between us. Using two fingers, I rubbed small harsh circles against her clit.

I needed her to come. I knew I wouldn't be able to hold on for much longer. Not with her hot skin rubbing against mine, the feel of her perfect pussy sucking me in, and the sweet sounds she made each time I hit that spot deep inside her.

The tingle in my spine began to unfurl as I increased the pressure and speed of my movements against her clit.

"Yes, gods, yes, don't stop Mal, don't fucking stop!" she screamed as her pussy tightened around me. Pinching her clit, Ashera tumbled over the edge. Her wings unfurled behind her, no longer hidden by the glamor as Ashera melted at my touch. Within seconds I exploded. I pushed through the wave of pleasure, pumping into her as hard as I could, being sure to draw out every drop of pleasure from both of us.

Resting my head against her shoulder, I caught my breath before lifting my gaze. I took a deep inhale before leaning in to kiss her.

"I love you Sher, and I've missed you too," I said between strokes of her lips against mine.

She laughed softly, her whole face lighting at the words that left me, before nibbling her lip and saying, "I love you too, Mal."

9

AMBROSE

I stood on a rise overlooking the castle I had once called home. Admittedly, the cold stone walls and even colder courtiers had never felt remotely safe or welcoming. Not the way that anywhere with Ashera felt. I found it ironic that I'd needed to travel so far, change so much, just to learn the true definition of the word home. The sleek, harsh structure was dark against the bleak backdrop, a perfectly miserable castle in a perfectly miserable place. The palace was pressed into the stone of the mountain, as though the rock had moved to make way for Masas' royalty. The spires stretched skyward, the points sharp and gleaming in the silvery sun. It was flashy, sure, shiny and flawlessly maintained, but, past the facade, it was hollow and bitter.

I glanced over at Ashera; her godsdamned cloak on again. Home wasn't a place. It was a person. She was home.

And I'd kill anyone who threatened her.

My fingers curled into tight fists as I returned my gaze back to the palace. My father had been the one to build the hideous structure—no surprise really. Looking at it now, I realized it was just as pointless as he was. Over the top and flashy with no real substance.

Gods. Just as I had been not that long ago. Shame crashed through me at the thought, but I brushed it back, knowing that I was no longer that vampire.

Small, delicate fingers slid against mine before squeezing gently. I looked down at my mate with a grin. She smiled back up at me.

"I know what happens next isn't going to be easy, Ambrose." Her voice is soft and serious.

"My people deserve a better leader," I said. "They deserve someone who will listen to them, someone who won't ignore the injustices going on around them."

Leaning up on her toes, she pressed a kiss to my cheek, surprising me. "I'm really proud of you, you know."

I blinked down at her for a minute before bringing our linked hands to my lips for a kiss. "Thank you, little queen. That means more than you will ever know."

"We think that Tomas is still in Sahira," Ashera said with a smile. "So you might run into some resistance, but we should be able to take care of those still loyal to him."

I nodded. Unfortunately, I was fairly certain that the majority of nobles were still very much loyal to my father. Why change a good thing? I sighed and ran my free hand through my hair. I had to hope that some secretly felt the way I now did, or that I could at least convince them to see things as we did. There was so much potential.

"We can do this," Malachi said as he approached, slapping a hand on my shoulder. "I'd hoped we could do this in a peaceful manner, but this isn't the first kingdom we've had to overthrow."

I wasn't entirely sure that made me feel better.

"Do you need to feed?" I asked Ashera, changing the subject.

She shook her head. "No. I didn't feed last night either."

I reared back. "Why not?"

"Ambrose, you remember when I did that little demonstration in Shaytan for you?" I did. I'd been hard as a fucking rock after, practically panting and begging to get in her leathers. "I can't do that if I'm too well fed, and we may need that in case things go sideways."

I studied her before turning my attention to Malachi. He was facing me with a serious expression on his face. Okay, then. He agreed.

I returned my focus to my mate. "Fine, but if you're running low at *any* time you either feed that way or you find me and drain me."

She scoffed. "Yes. Draining you of blood will surely make the people believe in you as their king." She rolled her eyes. "Don't worry, princess, I know how to handle myself."

I growled. "I'm going to redden your ass for that."

"Promises, promises," she taunted.

"If the two of you are done," Malachi interrupted, the cockblock. "Let's go meet up with Winta and Thorne. We've got a kingdom to conquer."

WE'D MADE the decision to have just Malachi and I head into the palace and address the court, but I was regretting that choice almost as soon as my feet crossed the threshold. I wouldn't put it past my father to make this a trap. He's probably film it the way he'd filmed Ashera's torture.

"Y-your Highness!" A servant came scurrying up, bowing deeply. "We hadn't received word of your imminent arrival. I apologize, nothing is ready for you."

"Is my father here?" I demanded.

"N-no. He hasn't been in the palace since you were last here." The servant shook his head.

"Gather the nobles. Now." I easily slid back into the role I played of the bloodthirsty prince. "I want the entire court in the throne room in thirty minutes or you're all dead. Am I clear?"

"Y-y-yes." With another deep bow, the servant scrambled away.

"Was that really necessary?" Malachi asked as we made our way to the throne room.

"Yes." I narrowed my eyes on him. "I can be a different ruler once I'm officially king, Mal. But right now, I need to make sure they don't scent weakness. If they do, they'll pounce.

"If you say so." He shrugged.

Irritation bubbled to life inside me, but I bit back my response as we entered the currently empty throne room. Unfortunately, it had been cleaned since I was last in here, but the items I'd destroyed hadn't been replaced. It was a start.

I fingered the obsidian blade strapped to my hip as I considered the space. There were now two thrones in the center of the room. One for my father, and a smaller one where I'd been placed if I ever made a public appearance with him. I'd always sat in that smaller throne in the past.

Not today. Never again.

I stepped up and slid into the large of the two thrones. Malachi nodded in approval and stood at my side. He folded his arms over his broad chest and the look on his face would make weak males run in fear.

The doors slammed open and the nobles started to flood into the room, most pausing in shock upon seeing me in my father's throne.

"What is the meaning of this?" Bastien, my father's closest ally in the court, demanded. He stood inches from the platform where the thrones stood with a scowl on his face and his hands fisted at his side. The other nobles around him went silent.

I let my power rise as my lips curled. The tension in the air thick-ened and several nobles took nervous steps back. Bastien wouldn't back down, I knew this. I *wanted* this.

"It's come to my attention that my father has been lacking in his official duties," I responded, keeping my tone bored. "As you're already aware, he's been incapable of performing this role as king for quite some time."

Many in the room shifted nervously as they waited for Bastien to respond. It seemed they'd elected him as their de facto leader. That wouldn't last long.

"King Tomas has never been more powerful," Bastien snarled.

I laughed and raised a brow. "Truly? Then why has he been ruling through me? Why has he been unable to confront me in person? If he were truly as powerful as you're claiming, he certainly wouldn't stand around and allow me to sit on his throne."

Bastien's eyes glowed and his face flushed with his anger. "He has been busy cleaning up *your* mess."

I glanced up at Malachi. "My mess? Did you know I'd made a mess?" I asked the incubus assassin.

It was the first time I'd drawn attention to him since the nobles had walked into the room. Several glanced at him and then around the room. Bastien's gaze narrowed on Mal, the hatred shining in his eyes had the incubus smirking at him.

"And you bring an outsider here. A member of the group that overthrew Shaytan's king!" Bastien jabbed a finger in Mal's direction.

"Yes, well, I've allied myself with him, you see." I shrugged my shoulders. "After all, we were mated to the same female."

Stunned silence greets my declaration.

"Oh come now," I taunted. "You mean to tell me rumors of the coup in Qamar and my part in it haven't reached Masas yet? I find that very hard to believe."

"Your Highness," a young noblewoman, Tamahra, stepped forward, shooting Bastien a glare. "We heard the rumors."

"Finally!" I leaned forward and clapped my hands. "Someone willing to speak the truth."

"Tamahra does not speak for the nobles, Ambrose." Several gasps rang out at Bastien's informal use of my name.

"Is that so, Bastien?" I placed my elbows on my knees to rest my head on my hands. "Why don't you enlighten me."

"We're well aware of your treasonous relationship with the whore of Shaytan." Malachi stiffened, but I refused to show any reaction. "We're well aware that you slaughtered your own people to protect the cunt. Your father needed to be sure of your alliance. Imagine his extreme shame to learn that you'd thrown your lot in with low-lives."

I flicked my eyes over the others gathered around the room. Some were nodding at what Bastien was saying, others were cowering and attempting to look as small as possible. So not all of the nobles believed as Bastian and my father, that was good.

"You further shamed him when he learned you'd played a part in overthrowing King Vaughn in Qamar," Bastien spat. "As such, King Tomas has given me the authority to place you and your...*allies* under arrest." He snapped his fingers. "Guards!"

The guards standing around the room shifted, and the doors around the throne room clanged open as soldiers flooded the space.

"So this is how it's to be?" I asked as the nobles around the room scrambled to press themselves against the walls.

"You're lucky King Tomas asked that I keep you alive." Bastien's voice rose above the noise. "I wanted to have you drawn and quartered here in the throne room."

"I see," I said quietly.

The soldiers continued their advance. I turned to nod at Malachi, who leaned down, grabbed my arm, and then took to the air. I clung to his arm as I gazed down at my subjects.

"Those of you that follow Bastien and my father will burn. If you want to live, you'll flee the city and play no part in the coming blood-bath," I yelled above the din of the soldiers below.

Mal flew us through a large window and away from the palace.

I hardened my heart against the knowledge that I was about to slaughter a good number of my people.

~

Thorne

I HADN'T any doubt in my mind that Ambrose had been walking into a trap. Hell, I'd tried to warn the bloodsucker against going in with just Malachi as backup. He'd insisted on going anyway. Idiot. I watched as they flew back to our basecamp, fighting the urge to yell 'I told you so!' as loud as I could.

Instead, I made my way to the command tent. We'd all convene there to discuss what had happened in the palace before they'd been forced to flee. Then we'd come up with a game plan to slaughter those assholes where they stood.

I pushed the door flap to the side and strode into the command tent. Ashera, Winta, and Bradford were standing around a large wooden table that had a detailed map of Masas on it.

"Where is Judah?" I asked, looking around to see if the creepy witch king was trying to hide in a corner somewhere.

"King Judah is taking a shit," Winta said. "I sent several guards with him. They just left."

I coughed on a laugh before nodding to Bradford. "Go keep an eye on all of them. I don't trust that fucker."

"Yes sir." Bradford immediately left the tent.

A moment later, Malachi and Ambrose burst through the entrance. The vampire prince looked ready to slaughter everyone that had ever made him angry, which probably included everyone in this tent. At least the incubus looked calm, if a little amused.

"So some asshole named Bastien seems to think that we should all be sucking Tomas's dick," Mal announced with a chuckle. "Honestly, if Bastien was any further up your father's ass--"

"I get it," Ambrose hissed in irritation. "I knew to expect shit from him, but for him to have control of the guards and soldiers like that...My father either gave the direct order himself, or he instilled some form of authority on Bastien before he left."

"He said Tomas had given him permission," Malachi pointed out.

"That could have been a lie." Ambrose waved a dismissive hand.

"Care to fill the rest of us in?" Ashera asked as she walked up to both males. She ran a hand along both of them, as though assuring herself they were safe and whole before returning to the table.

"Ambrose declaring himself king went about as well as we expected." Mal shrugged and propped a hip against the table, studying the map as he spoke. Ambrose growled. "It's true, princess. Get over yourself. We went in there knowing there was almost no chance we'd be walking out of there after a nice little chat. You knew we'd need to fight."

"Just because I knew it, doesn't mean it sits well with me, you fucker," Ambrose snarled. "I'm about to send an army in to slaughter my people."

That had all of us stopping in our tracks. He was right. We'd all killed our own people, but that didn't mean it was an easy choice to make. I shouldn't be surprised that Ambrose was struggling with the decision. Innocents shouldn't have to die because those with more political power were too stupid to stand down.

"But you warned those who weren't in league with Bastien and your father to try to get out of the city. Even if they don't leave, hopefully they at least stay out of the way." Malachi continued to study the map before turning his gaze to Ambrose. "What's the best way into the city?"

"I can't believe I'm doing this," Ambrose sighed as he approached the table. "There are several hidden entrances that will allow us multiple points of entry. Some of them Bastien will know about, but others...*Fuck!*" He slammed his hands down on the table, frustration clear on his face. "My father has probably told Bastien about all of the entrances. So I'm sure we can expect to meet resistance no matter where we enter the city."

"How many men?" Judah asked as he strode back into the tent, Bradford on his heels. "Surely not all of Masas's army will be in the city?"

"You sound just as idiotic as you look," Ambrose snapped. "You've interacted with my father, are you honestly this dense?"

Judah scowled at the vampire before assuming a spot between myself and Malachi. "I clearly don't know him as well as you do."

Ambrose laughed. "I'm sure that's what you want us to believe."

I rubbed my temples. "Enough. Ambrose, Judah is here to help."

"Sure." The vampire turned back to gazing at the map.

"Okay," I said, returning my attention to the map as well. "Knowing that we're likely to encounter soldiers no matter where we enter the city, which ones are the easiest for us to push our way through?"

Ambrose started pointing to different areas around the city. "We'll be able to easily fan out once we get inside. These spots are pretty hard to defend, which is why only the royal family knows about them."

I nodded, paying close attention as a plan formed slowly. It was odd, though reassuring, how easily we planned together, Ashera and Ambrose leading the conversation while the rest of us chipped in with suggestions. It felt natural. Perhaps it should have unnerved me, but when I looked up from the map and caught Ashera's eyes, the soft smile playing on her lips as she looked over us all, happiness washed over me. True, we were gearing up for battle, but I'd never felt more like I belonged.

Talk of strategy wound down, tensions between Judah and Ambrose still high. Ashera had moved to ignoring both of them, watching Mal, her green eyes narrowed.

"If you wouldn't mind, I need some time alone with my inner circle," she said to Judah and Bradford, pointedly keeping her attention on Malachi.

Judah opened his mouth to protest, but Ambrose was at his side in an instant, ushering him out. She waited until we could no longer hear his footsteps before speaking.

"Do you need to feed?" Ashera asked Mal, cocking her head to the side to analyze him. He narrowed his eyes on her, the energy in the room immediately thickening.

"I'm fine," he answered, focus solely on her as she shook her head in response, already beginning to strip her leathers.

"Don't lie to me," she said, rolling her eyes as he tensed, but didn't object further.

Fuck. I watched, unable to look anywhere but her, as she undressed torturously slowly, my dick already painfully hard. I was still furious that Ambrose's jealousy hadn't let me near my mate, the scent of her arousal driving me insane as she finally stood bare before us. I stalked toward her, pulling her attention from Mal and grabbing her waist, tugging her against me.

I groaned, gripping her ass and lifting her up to sit her on the table, spreading her thighs so I could stand between them. The map rustled beneath her but I didn't care. My cock pressed against her leg as I leaned in, tilting her head back to capture her mouth and groaning at the taste of her. I'd never needed anything more than I needed her. The distance between us was driving me insane, the need to complete our bond, to finally fucking know what it felt like to be buried inside her, pushing me closer to the edge of my sanity.

"Fuck, kitten," I groaned, palming her tits and relishing in the little moans she gave me in return. I dragged one hand lower, my mate spreading her thighs wider instinctively, arching into my touch despite the anger I could feel radiating off the vampire as he watched us. I didn't care. I dragged my fingers over her drenched pussy, laughing darkly as she bucked her hips against me, begging to be fucked.

Gladly. I reached for my cock, desperate to feel her around me, as I dragged her arousal up to her clit, circling it with my thumb as she panted.

"I don't fucking think so, you overgrown cat," a familiar, unwelcome voice interrupted, the accompanying hand on my shoulder pulling me away from my mate. The second I stopped touching her, she blinked, a mixture of guilt and annoyance flitting over her perfect features. "We can take perfectly good care of our mate without you tearing her apart with that thing."

His obsession with my cock should be flattering. I growled, pissed at being taken from Ashera, but one look from her and I knew not to fight it. Mal needed to feed, and she needed to smooth things out with the moody vamp before she'd let me fuck her senseless in the way I knew we both craved.

Resigned to watching, albeit unhappy about it, I lowered myself into a chair, tugging my leathers down so my cock sprung free fully. Ambrose had immediately taken up my place, kneeling before her and feasting on her like a starved man, his head between her legs blocking my fucking view. Winta was at her side in an instant, running her hands over her body, rolling her peaked nipples between her fingers as she kissed her neck. Ashera's head was tipped back in pleasure, lips parted in a soft moan as the vamp sucked on her clit and Winta continued to play with her tits, Ashera's hands fisted in the map beneath her, nails tearing through the paper and shredding the depiction of the castle.

Mal moved quickly from his place by the table, grabbing her hair to angle her toward him, kissing her as hungrily as Ambrose was eating her out. She whined, the sound needy and filled with desire, and I fisted my cock, unable to stave off the urge to join any longer. I may not be able to touch my mate, but I knew she was able to sense what I was doing, the pleasure I got from watching her come apart.

"Ambrose," she moaned, bucking against his face as he speared two fingers inside her without once moving his mouth from her clit. Winta grinned against her skin, sucking on the pulse point at her neck, working with Malachi and Ambrose to drive her closer to the edge.

Jealousy reared its head inside me, the desire to join them burning through me, nearly impossible to ignore. But I would fight it. She wouldn't get my dick until she talked with Ambrose, no matter how much I knew she wanted it.

"Come all over his tongue, little slut," Mal encouraged, swallowing her cries as she obeyed his command, practically riding the vampire's face as she came.

Gods, I could watch her forever. I ached to be there, feeling her orgasm take over her, tasting her moans on her tongue.

Before she could recover, Mal flipped her, dragging her off the table to the floor and urging her onto her hands and knees. She was shaking slightly but held herself still as Mal dragged a chair over and offered it to Winta. She frowned at him, but sat in front of our mate, Ashera's head level with her legs.

Our mate sat up, ignoring the demon's growl, stripping Winta of her leathers until she was bared to Ashera. Immediately, she pulled Winta to the edge of the chair, so Ashera's head was between the shifter queen's legs as my kitten returned to her position, appeasing Malachi once more.

"You're going to make Winta come while you take my cock in that perfect pussy and Ambrose fucks your ass," he told her, leaving no room for arguments. Ashera's gaze met mine, lids heavy and pupils blown with lust. Mal's eyes followed, narrowing on me as his lips curved up in a smirk. "And Thorne watches. Take notes, *kitten.*"

I stood, anger burning to the surface. I'd fucking show him how well I could take care of her pussy. When I finally got my hands on her, she'd be a mess by the time we were done--

"Don't even fucking think about it, kitty cat," Ambrose taunted, glaring at me. "Keep that mutant dick over there."

I growled, the desire to tear the blood-sucking bastard limb from limb almost too painful to ignore. My mate pinned me with a look, shaking her head as if warning me not to test them right now. I understood, tensions were high and Mal needed to feed, but fuck, it was pissing me off to be excluded *yet again.*

Soon. I'd get her alone soon.

Malachi shed his clothes quickly and maneuvered so he was beneath Ashera, Ambrose behind her with her face still buried between Winta's thighs as she teased the dragon shifter with long, slow licks.

"Ride our cocks, little slut," the incubus urged as Ambrose shoved his own leathers down and coated his dick with lube, sliding a finger into her ass to prepare her before beginning to press into her.

"Fuck, she's so tight," the vampire ground out, no doubt just to piss me off.

She moaned, the sound followed closely by Winta's as Ashera sought out her clit, patience apparently gone.

Malachi wasted no time, lining himself up with her soaking entrance before sheathing himself in one thrust, causing her to cry out again, the sound muffled by Winta's thighs.

They fucked the gorgeous succubus without mercy, Ashera moving with them without a second thought, chasing the pleasure I could fucking *see* coursing through her.

Fuck. I worked my hand over my ridged dick, my body desperate for relief. I'd never imagined that watching my mate be taken by two other men, and eating out my best friend, would turn me on so fucking much but any situation with Ashera made me hard. She was irresistible. The need I felt for her would surely only grow stronger once I'd had a taste of her.

Winta came first as Ashera closed her mouth over her clit, drawing out every last drop of pleasure from her mate. She pulled back as Winta came down from the high, licking her lips to catch every drop Winta gave her. My mate's eyes locked on mine as she grinned, pleasure and satisfaction clear on her face. The sight ruined me, and I followed, immediately regretting not stripping completely when come soaked the front of my shirt. Ashera's moans grew louder as she watched me, Mal's pace increasing.

"Make her come, Ambrose," Malachi demanded through clenched teeth, gripping her hips to hold her still as he fucked her harder. "Come on my dick, little slut."

From my angle, I nearly missed the way the vampire reached around her and pinched her clit, but there was no missing the way her orgasm hit her. Her back arched, hips pushing against Ambrose's, her breathy moans filling the air as she shook. He cursed as she fell forward, slamming into her ass once more before his orgasm hit, shoving them flat against Mal's chest as pleasure wrecked them both.

Malachi cursed as he came, slamming into her hard and groaning as she panted, her nails digging into his chest as she cling to him.

Jealousy spiked again as they separated and cleaned up, Winta holding Ashera close and kissing her softly. Malachi, admittedly, looked better for having fed. I swallowed the sting of the bitter emotion, crossing to Ashera and pressing my lips to hers before Ambrose could yank her off Winta and stop me. The soft reassurance of her mouth against mine calmed the riot inside me, soothing the ache I felt for her.

I could only hope Ambrose got his shit together and realized that this was as hard on her as it was on me and stopped obsessing over my dick long enough to put her first.

10

AMBROSE

I was still battling with myself over killing Masas's people, but I knew this was the right decision. No one in Masas could ever truly be free if the kingdom continued to practice slavery.

That thought struck me.

The nobility were trapped in a corrupt and unjust system, one built on the backs of mortal slaves. Until we liberated the mortals, those that were too blinded by a diseased system would remain trapped, unable to see freedom for the gift it was. To everyone.

"I know this is a stupid question," Ashera said as she stepped out of the tent after me. I'd left after we'd agreed on a means of attack, needing air. Needing to think. "Are you okay?"

I laughed, wrapping an arm around her shoulders and pulling her tight against me. "I'm not sure," I replied honestly.

"Fair." She leaned into my touch and rested her head against me. "Will you tell me if you're not feeling okay?"

"I can do that," I assured her. "I don't know if I'm quite self-aware enough to know for sure..."

"Hey." She placed her hand on my cheek, soothing me. "Just let me know whenever you know, okay?"

I leaned down to press a kiss to her forehead. "I promise."

"I'll be honest," she started. "I hadn't really thought about the fact that I was killing the people I would one day rule over. I was mostly focused on revenge and rage. I don't regret killing those that sincerely stood with the former king, but I do harbor some guilt over innocents that were caught in the middle."

"How do you deal with the guilt?"

"I do my best to honor their memory." Ashera's answer was whispered quietly. "I attempt to give back using what I have gained."

"I shall try to do the same," I vowed.

"I know you will." She smiled up at me. "You're a good male, Ambrose."

"Because of you, little queen."

Footsteps behind us had us both looking over our shoulders. Winta, Thorne, Malachi, Judah, and Bradford made their way over to us. It was time. Any reservations I had vanished, at least for now. Now, I needed to focus on winning this battle so I could claim Masas, free its slaves, and be one step closer to finding and killing my father. One step closer to securing Ashera's safety. One step closer to assuring our future together.

"Are you ready?" Winta asked, her eyes scanning my face. "The men we have in the air have reported seeing them mobilize in the city, so we should head out now if we want to push any advantage."

I nodded.

"Mal and Bradford will stay with Ashera during the initial surge. We want to keep her a secret for as long as possible, and you're their main target right now let's keep it that way," Thorne explained.

Ashera nodded then looked up at me. "Don't you dare die. If you die I will find a way to bring you back before killing you myself."

I chuckled. "Of course, little queen. I wouldn't think of dying on you."

Mal, Bradford, and Ashera left to join their squadron, leaving me with Thorne, Winta, and Judah. Fucking witch king scum. I know the others wanted to make it seem like we'd accepted him into the fold, but I just couldn't do it. Everything about the asshole was off and screamed traitor.

I was also sick of pretending. I've had to pretend to be someone else my entire life, and after everything that has happened with Ashera...I just couldn't pretend anymore. Living as my true self, learning who I really am...that has been the most valuable lesson. *No one should ever have to live as anything other than who they truly are.* That was a thought worth fighting and dying for.

Winta shot Thorne a look, and he ushered Judah away. I turned to the shifter queen with a raised brow.

"I wanted to talk to you," Winta started. "I know how hard this must be for you. I faced a similar situation not that long ago. I figured you could use someone to talk to."

I studied Ashera's newest mate, a swell of respect crested in me. "I'd actually like that."

Winta smiled. "I know it's not easy to put words to your emotions, but even just rambling might help."

"How did you come to terms with it? Knowing that you'd need to kill some of your people to free others?" I inquired.

"I still haven't," she confessed. "It's a decision that weighs on me every single day. But what you ultimately need to think about is this: can you live with yourself if you do nothing?"

I rocked back on my heels. Could I live with myself if I did nothing? The answer came surprisingly easy. No. I sure as fuck wouldn't be able to live with myself if I did nothing.

Reading my expression, Winta nodded her head. "Exactly. The loss of life is exponentially higher if you do nothing, Ambrose."

"You're right," I admitted.

"So now you need to ask yourself what you want to do to ensure the betterment of your people." She canted her head.

"I want to burn it all." My voice surprised me as it burst from my chest. "I want all those who would harm others for their own greed to flood the streets with their blood before I burn it all to ash."

"As you wish," Winta said with a bow of her head, "my King."

As I approached the entrance assigned to me, I could already hear the shouts and screams of battle, the clashing thunder of steel against steel, smell the metallic tang of blood in the air, the pungent sting of piss. I paused for a moment to take a deep inhale. I needed to give myself over to my bloodlust to do this properly.

So I released the hold I had on my vampiric nature. My inner beast roared to the surface as the ground beneath my feet started to tremble with my power. Unlike the fae, this shaking wasn't caused by elemental magic. It was caused by the sheer force of power flying through every nerve ending in my body. I could feel my eyes as they started to glow and my fangs lengthen past my lower lip. My nails became sharper, my muscles felt packed with power. My senses sharpened.

My hunger flooded me. My eyes blinked slowly as a cruel smile curled my lips. I would feast until I couldn't hold anymore, then I would paint the buildings red.

The muscles in my legs coiled as I prepared to launch myself into the battle, reveling in the screams as our troops tore through the vampires attempting--in vain--to defend my father's property...*my property*. I purred as I collided with a young soldier, my fangs easily sinking into his cheek. Hot, power-filled blood surged into my mouth as his pained scream rent the air around us.

For a moment, all I could focus on was the pounding rhythm of his frantically beating heart, the tangy, fear-soaked taste of his blood, the power that threatened to rip me apart, the feel of his flesh as it tore beneath my fingertips, the crunch of his bones as they snapped due to the force of my hold.

All of it was an aphrodisiac so much stronger than any succubus pheromone.

Far too soon, there was no blood left within the soldier's withered husk. Pity. I released the desiccated carcass, and it fell to the ground with a soft thud, already on the hunt for my next victim.

I loved a bloody battlefield.

I licked the blood off my fingers as I spotted my next target. One of the nobles who thought that standing with my father would garner him respect and power.

Allowing him one small glance at me before I struck, I grinned as my fingers closed around his still beating heart. The muscle contracted. Once...Twice...I closed my fist and basked in the spray of blood that coated me as I ripped the organ from his chest. His large, shocked eyes held mine as I lifted the now pulpy meat to my fangs. Never once breaking eye contact as I ripped each chamber apart, blood smearing over my face and down my chest.

Finally, his legs gave way beneath him. His back smacked against the cobblestones. I flung the useless organ away from me, laughing at the sound of its wet slap against a nearby wall. Then I studied the dead noble at my feet, not bothering to clean myself of the blood and gore that now covered me.

I leaned down, gripped his hair in one hand and his shoulder in another. I pulled. It was pathetic how easy it was to divest this annoying gnat of his head. Holding the severed head above my own, I roared into the crowd. The fighting paused for mere seconds before resuming, but that was enough time for me to hurl the head into the masses of the enemy.

Let them see me coming for them. Let them fear me.

~

Malachi

WE'D MET some resistance as we entered the city, but not as much as I'd expected based on the encounter Ambrose and I had earlier in the palace. My mind screamed this was a trap, that something was wrong. This was far too fucking easy.

"Sher, stay with me," I barked as we made our way deeper into the city. "Bradford, you don't let Ashera out of your sight, do you understand?"

"Yes, sir!" Bradford covered Ashera's back as I covered her front. Even though he wasn't part of our merry little band, I trusted him to make sure that nothing snuck up on us.

"Mal," Ashera admonished.

"Not now, Sher."

Silence greeted me, but I could feel her irritation radiating off of her in waves. I'm not sure how we managed to make it this far into the city, but the entrance we'd come through hadn't been as well guarded as Ambrose assumed.

I could still hear the cries of battle and smell the blood that had already been spilled. We'd fought a small force not far back, but we hadn't encountered too many soldiers since. While it was possible that Bastien and his thugs had focused their soldiers on other entrances to the city, given what happened in the hinterlands, I wouldn't put it past them to ambush us. At least we had the witch king in case any of those assholes made an appearance today.

I slammed to a stop. Winta, Thorne, and Judah were directly in front of me, fighting off soldiers. There was no sign of Ambrose with them. I felt a small twinge of worry.

Until a roar rose above the cacophony of battle, drawing all of our attention--including the vampiric soldiers'--to one of the rooves overhead.

Ambrose stood on the edge of the roof, a severed head in one hand and a severed arm in the other. He kicked a large mass that then toppled down to the street in front of me. No blood splattered out of the lifeless corpse as it landed with a sickening thud. He then heaved the arm and head into the crowd of enemy soldiers, all of whom scattered.

"I'm finding this oddly arousing," Ashera whispered to me, her hand gripping mine. "And I mean like...*really* arousing."

I choked back a laugh. Of course she did.

"Are you done?" I called, keeping my eyes on the seemingly feral vampire above us.

Ambrose turned to look down at us. His movements were more fluid than I'd ever seen them, and it was clear that he was the definition of predator in this moment. I wasn't sure Ambrose was home, now that I studied him more closely.

"Bradford, take Ashera back a few steps." I held my arms out to keep the two of them behind me.

Since the soldiers that had been fighting the others had scattered when Ambrose threw a head at them, they approached slowly, eyeing the semi-crazed vampire. Ashera, thankfully, didn't protest as Bradford moved to place her between him and a wall. Ambrose, however, didn't seem to appreciate the move at all.

A roar once again speared the air seconds before Ambrose materialized in front of me, attempting to reach for Ashera. He snarled viciously at me before turning his attention to Bradford. Thorne's arms slammed down around Ambrose in a vice grip as I moved myself squarely between the feral bloodsucker and our mate.

"*Mine*," Ambrose snarled, his gaze still locked over my shoulder on Bradford, who was effectively blocking Ashera from view.

"Ours," I reminded him in a cheery tone.

"How do we snap him out of this?" Thorne asked through gritted teeth. It was clear the shifter was struggling to contain the vampire prince.

"This is some sort of souped-up bloodlust," I said as I studied Ambrose.

"You alright back there, kitten?" Thorne asked Ashera. She'd been pretty quiet up until now.

"I'm fine." Her voice was soft and soothing.

"*MINE!*" Ambrose roared.

We all stiffened. Thorne grunted as he strained to keep Ambrose contained.

~

Ashera

FERAL AMBROSE, at least at first, had been sexy as hell. But now...Now, I needed him to snap out of it. I needed *Ambrose* back. I felt Malachi's unease thanks to my emphatic gifts, and they fed my own feelings. There was something off about how empty the city was.

Did the vampires know that Ambrose could lose control of himself like this? Were they waiting for a moment like this to happen so they could strike? Perhaps they were hoping he would turn on us. Could he?

I shook my head. No. Ambrose wouldn't turn on us, even like this. He'd come a long way since we'd first met. I refused to believe that all of our trials together had been for naught. Ambrose, *my* Ambrose, was still in there.

I was frustrated because I couldn't see him. I understood that Malachi and the others wanted to keep me safe--they weren't sure what feral Ambrose was capable of--but they needed to trust in my bond with Ambrose. I could bring him out of this. I just needed his full attention and for the others to let me handle this.

Peeking over Bradford's shoulder, I made eye contact with Ambrose.

In the next instant, Ambrose had Bradford's head tilted, his fangs plunged deep into the shifter's neck, ruby eyes glowing dangerously at me. In a horrified slow-motion, I watched as Ambrose ripped his mouth from Bradford's neck, tearing it out in the process.

I screamed.

"R-run, Ash," Bradford rasped in a whisper thin voice.

My hands rose to my face of their own volition as blood sprayed over it, the steaming liquid shocking me more than the sight in front of me. It made what was happening all the more real.

Bradford's next gurgling breath broke me out of my stupor. I launched into action, my hands reaching for the shifter's arms as his legs started to give way.

"I've got you," I chanted over and over again.

A viciously feral snarl was the only warning I received before Bradford was ripped from my arms.

"No!" I yelled at Ambrose, lunging after my injured friend. "Ambrose, don't!"

"*Mine!*" His roar was followed by another spray of blood and the sound of ripping flesh and breaking bones.

My mind struggled to process the scene before me. Ambrose stood, bathed in Bradford's blood...holding a bloody spine. Bradford was crumpled in a heap at my vampire's feet, his open eyes already clouding over, pain etched on his features.

I dropped to my knees, my hands running over Bradford's body as my mind went blank, a buzzing filling my ears.

"No, no, no, no," I chanted. "I can fix this, Bradford. I promise I can fix this."

Ambrose ripped me from Bradford's body, the shifter's spine still held in one hand as the other lifted me and slammed me against the wall at my back. He held the spine in front of my face before he threw it behind him, moving his face inches from mine.

"*Mine,*" he snarled.

Ambrose was yanked away from me with a bellow of rage as Malachi came swimming into view. My heart pounded in my chest, my mind not yet fully realizing what just happened, my chest heaving with each breath I took. It was only when Mal took my hands that I realized I was shaking.

"Sher," Malachi demanded. "Sher. Look at me."

My gaze finally focused on Mal's face as tears burned and fought to break free. Keeping a death grip on one hand, he moved the other to cup my bloody cheek, concern oozing from his gaze.

"I need you to focus on me, Ashera," my rock demanded.

The sound of flesh pounding against flesh, snarls, growls, and shouts rent the air. I fought to keep my gaze centered on Malachi.

"Winta!" Mal called over his shoulder. "Come to Ashera so I can help with Ambrose."

My free hand gripped Mal's forearm, bringing his attention back to me.

"I need to bring him back," I said in a soft, quiet voice.

A thunderous look crossed Malachi's face, rage radiating both down the bond and through my empathic gifts. "Absolutely not."

"I'm here." Winta's soft, soothing voice had both of us looking at her as she took Malachi's place in front of me. He didn't say another word and left us standing together.

"He killed Bradford," I whispered. "I *let* him kill Bradford."

"Stop that right now, precious," Winta snapped. "That's bullshit and you know it. You didn't let Ambrose do anything."

"How the hell are you so calm about this?" I demanded.

"Because I have a dual nature. My dragon can get out of control," she explained. "I've killed people I shouldn't have, all because I couldn't control my dragon. What Ambrose did... He's going to live with that for the rest of his life."

"Gods," I breathed. "Ambrose will be crushed when he's himself again."

I gazed up at Winta through burning eyes. I wouldn't let the tears fall. Not yet. Not while Ambrose still needed help. I wouldn't let the resistance take another person from me, especially not one of my mates.

That was who was truly to blame for Bradford's death. The resistance. We could have peacefully negotiated, but they chose violence. They chose to start a war. They chose to send innocents off to die for them instead of taking care of matters themselves.

They were everything that was wrong in Dunya.

And I was going to reduce them to ashes.

"If we don't at least let him near her, he's going to kill us both!" Thorne bellowed, drawing my attention past Winta to where Judah, Thorne, and Malachi were struggling to contain a still very feral Ambrose.

"He won't hurt me," I called back. "He had the opportunity."

"We're not going to just let him at you!" Malachi objected.

"Then come over here with him," I snapped.

A long moment of silence followed before Ambrose was once again in front of me. Malachi and Thorne flanked him.

Ambrose stood before me, his arms pinned to his side once more by Thorne's immovable hold. His eyes, which usually shone with warmth and love, still gleamed with the ruby red coldness of the killer we now knew he could be. Nothing of my loving mate reflected back at me.

Bruises dusted his face from the beating Mal and Thorne had given him. Watching my mates fight for dominance wasn't new, but usually it was done to please me.

Never had they fought to prevent one from killing. It had taken everything in me to stand still and watch as they rained punch after punch upon Ambrose.

I flinched at the sight of his blood oozing from his chin. One of the hits had caught his jaw, and Ambrose had cut himself off of his still extended fangs.

Everything about my mate screamed that he was a predator at that moment. Even beaten and bloody he still fought to reach me. I watched as his muscles flexed beneath Thorne's hold, trying to break free. I knew that he wouldn't, that Thorne would rather lose an arm than let Ambrose go. He wouldn't risk my safety, not when they were so worried about his current state.

I reached out to grab his hand but paused at the sight of the blood coating them. It was Bradford's blood. Brushing the thought aside I returned my focus to my mate. He needed me.

I could faintly see bruises beginning to form beneath the blood caked and cracking across his ivory skin. His hands, the same hands that had been used to please me again and again, had instead been transformed into weapons.

His nails were longer, sharper, and coated in blood and chunks of gods knew what.

His chest heaved, nostrils flaring with each inhale he took. His ruby eyes continued to glow eerily as they absorbed every inch of me. The low growl that emanated from his chest was heated. It was a clear statement of his intent.

"He doesn't want to hurt me," I reiterated. "He wants to fuck me."

Thorne released a disgruntled snarl. "After what he just did—"

"I'm well aware of what he just did, Thorne," I snapped, not taking my eyes off my vampire prince. "But he needs help to get back to himself. If this is what he needs, this is what he's going to get."

Thankfully, my feline shifter didn't argue with me. Malachi knew me well enough by now to know that it was pointless to argue this point, and I had a feeling he thought this was perhaps our best option of getting Ambrose out of his bloodlust.

"You two can help. Make sure that I'm safe," I added.

Surprisingly, Ambrose had allowed our exchange without protest. He simply continued to study me with a hungry look. I realized there would be no foreplay, no teasing touches, or taunting verbal sparring to accompany this joining. No. This was going to be hard and fast, animalistic in every way.

I wasn't opposed to the idea.

To ensure that everyone was ready for what was about to happen, I released my pheromones into the air, grateful when Malachi immediately followed suit. Then slowly, carefully, I raised my hands to Ambrose's face. He leaned into my touch with a purr of contentment. Thorne eased his grip to allow my vampire prince to move closer to me.

"Okay, big buy. I'm going to let you do what you need to do, but if this doesn't bring *my* Ambrose back...I'm going to fuck you up." I kept my voice stern as I pulled his face closer to mine. "And it isn't going to be enjoyable for either of us."

Before he could rip my leathers off my body, I removed my hands from his face and made quick work of removing them. Winta grabbed them and moved them out of harm's way. Bless her.

Thorne, clearly not wanting to be left out again, stripped himself as Ambrose shredded his clothes in his haste to get to me. Malachi moved to the side, content to watch, at least for the time being.

Ambrose leaned in and pressed his body against mine, not even noticing when Thorne gripped his hips from behind. *Gods, Thorne is going to fuck Ambrose.*

In the blink of an eye, Ambrose lifted me by my legs and slammed into me. A harsh cry of pleasure ripped from my throat. Thorne didn't waste any time. He wrapped an arm around Ambrose's neck before thrusting into my vampire from behind, causing the male trapped between us to groan long and loud.

"More," Ambrose grumbled, starting to sound more like himself.

"More," I agreed.

With that, Ambrose and Thorne set a brutal pace. The sound of flesh slapping against flesh filled the street, punctuated only by a moan, groan, or cry from one of us.

The hand not anchoring Ambrose to Thorne's chest, snaked around to play with my clit. My head fell back with a thud against the wall at my back. All I could do was ride each wave of pleasure as it came, bringing me closer and closer to the edge.

The sharp sting of Ambrose's fangs as they sank into my neck sent me over, and I screamed as I came, clenching tightly around my vampire. Ambrose roared his release around my neck moments later, followed closely by Thorne's bellow.

Panting, sweaty, and still clinging to one another, Ambrose lifted his head. His features had smoothed back to normal, concern shining in his stunning ruby eyes.

"A-Ashera?" The question in his tone almost broke me.

"It's okay, Ambrose," I soothed. "I'm okay."

Thorne pulled out of Ambrose and backed away to shuck on his clothes. Ambrose stood, holding me as the events of the past several hours replayed in his mind. I could see the horror start to form, and my heart broke a little more.

Gently placing me on my feet, Ambrose strode away from us, his hands running through his hair before tugging at the ends. He was still covered in blood, still marked by what he'd done. Watching his mind catch up was the most horrible part of this.

"Ambrose." I kept my tone soft and soothing. "Ambrose, this wasn't your fault."

"I am no better than that monster!" He cried. "I killed an innocent man!" He thrusted a finger in Bradford's direction.

I quickly dressed and grabbed what was left of his pants as I slowly approached my vampire. This wasn't going to be easy on him. I could see how devastated he was by his actions. I wanted to take the pain away.

"Ambrose," I said in warning. "That is bullshit and you know it. Did you kill him? Yes. But you weren't aware of what you were doing at the time. You were lost to your bloodlust."

"That doesn't matter!" he yelled, holding his hands out in front of him to stop me from getting too close. "Stay back. I refuse to hurt you."

"You haven't. Even while in the throws of your bloodlust. You only wanted to mate with me, cement our bond." I tossed him his pants. He caught them and pulled them on. "Being with me brought you back. I know you won't hurt me."

"I can't right now, little queen." Gods, he sounded...dead. "I can't."

He was gone, taking off down the street. I held my arms out on either side of me, not letting the others go after him. If he needed time, we'd give it to him.

"Mal, have someone with wings watch over him, but leave him be for a while," I commanded. "Let's finish this battle. Then we can show Ambrose the truth."

With solemn nods, Malachi took off to get someone to watch over Ambrose while Throne, Winta, and Judah led me further into the battle. We'd make sure that my mate was safe, but we'd give him some time to process what had happened without too much pushing.

11

ASHERA

I t was difficult leaving Ambrose to fight against his own people by himself. I wanted nothing more than to be fighting by his side, especially after what he'd just gone through. But it wasn't my place to tell someone how to process their emotions, so I had to let this play out. I had to turn my focus back to freeing Masas from the stranglehold of an insane monster.

Once we made it to the heart of the city, I turned to look at the others, Malachi having just rejoined us a moment ago.

"This isn't right," I said.

"There's no one here," Mal replied.

We all turned to study our surroundings. Some of our soldiers poured into the center with us, but there was no sign of more vampires.

My heart rate sped up, making it feel as though the organ was about to gallop straight out of my chest. My fingers twitched around the daggers I held. The silence was deafening.

A single scream rose in the air, quickly followed by another, and another, until the roar of screams was almost too loud to think over.

"What the hell is happening?" I demanded.

Malachi shot into the sky. I was half tempted to follow him, but I knew that drawing attention to myself now wouldn't be wise. So I allowed my gaze to track my demonic mate as he gained altitude.

A flash of movement drew my attention from Mal. I breathed a sigh of relief when I realized it was Ambrose coming to join our ranks. He approached cautiously, as though he wasn't sure how he'd be received. Stupid male.

"Thank the gods you're okay," I said with a smile. He just grunted in response. "I'll address that issue later. Mal just took off to see what's going on."

"We're surrounded, that's what's going on," Ambrose snarled. "Bastien, that asshole, he held back most of his forces. If we're going to make it out of this alive, we're going to need to fight our way through."

Mal landed and tucked his wings close to his back. "The soldiers we have here with us now are all that are left. They've slaughtered everyone else."

I felt my face drain of color, memories of the hinterlands flooding my mind. We'd barely made it out of there, how could we possibly get all these soldiers out safely? I didn't dare to ask how many we were up against, their grim faces told me everything I needed to know.

We were going to die here.

Taking a deep breath, I turned to the others. They'd heard what Ambrose and Malachi had said, they knew what we faced. Surprisingly, Judah seemed to be the most calm out of all of us. I'd expected the little cowardly fucker to want to run for the hills.

That screamed red flag.

My eyes narrowed as I held Judah's gaze. If he was this calm about all of us getting slaughtered, that meant he'd known what was going to happen. Had he come to Qamar in the hopes of getting taken?

My legs moved without permission, slamming my feet against the cobblestones as I ate up the distance between us. The witch king took an alarmed step back as I got up in his face.

"What the fuck do you know?" I seethed. "Tell us right now before I slice off your pathetic excuse for a cock."

"How do we know he even has one?" Ambrose asked.

"He probably doesn't," Thorne agreed.

Judah scowled at the two of them before returning his attention back to me. "I don't know what you're talking about."

My hand snapped around his throat, causing his eyes to bulge as panic filled his gaze. "Do. Not. Fuck. With. Me."

"I'd listen to her," Winta chimed in happily. "If you thought Ambrose in bloodlust was bad..." She tsked.

Possibly too soon for an Ambrose in bloodlust comment, but I liked the way my mate thought.

"I have no idea what you're insinuating," Judah gasped out.

Just as I cocked my arm back to break this fucker's nose, more screams rang out around us as the vampires attacked. I shook the infuriating witch king before releasing him.

"I will deal with you later," I snapped. "Everyone keep at least one eye on this fucker. I want answers out of him when we make it out of this alive."

Everyone nodded, Thorne even going so far as to walk over to Judah and sling an arm around the witch king's shoulders. My sabertooth shifter was so getting laid after this.

We all turned to face the fighting as our soldiers closed ranks around us. This was it. I shuffled into the center and shot Malachi a look.

"It's not going to be easy to determine who is friend and who is foe," I yelled at him. "Keep as many of our people close as you can. I won't be able to drain them all, but I'm going to try to take out as many as possible."

"Sher," Mal responded, worry in his voice. "If you take too much..."

"I know," I acknowledged. "But this might be the only way to get us all out of here alive."

"What the fuck is going on?" Winta yelled over at us.

"Nothing!" I responded quickly, shooting Malachi a warning glare.

Taking a deep breath, I closed my eyes. I allowed my senses to expand, grounding myself as my awareness heightened enough that I could feel everyone's emotions all at once. It was too much, so I shut that gift down. Dropping my hands to my side, I took another deep breath before spreading my awareness to those who meant us harm.

Then I started to drain their energy.

It quickly became apparent that I was still far too well fed to take much from our enemies, despite not having fed during any of our recent bouts. I cursed, but continued to suck as much power as I could. Unfortunately, it didn't seem to be making much of a dent. The screams and sounds of fighting were getting too close.

I heard Ambrose shout a warning to Mal. I needed to focus. Needed to continue draining as much of the enemy as possible.

Time seemed to slow. My breaths became sluggish, and my body felt heavy. So heavy. My thoughts slowed to a crawl. My hearing tunneled. I was taking too much.

"Ashera!" Malachi cried as he shook some sense back into me. "Godsdammit Ashera! Stop!"

My eyes snapped open, green clashing with honey brown as we stared at one another. I let out a shaky breath before nodding my head.

"I'm okay," I assured.

"Like fuck you are," he snarled. "Stop. You're going to kill yourself."

"If I expel it all now—"

"Do it." He didn't leave room for negotiation.

He took a step back before turning to the ongoing battle, drawing his sword and launching himself at the nearest opponent.

That was my cue. I knelt against the cobblestones, placing my palms down on the slick surface. I needed to use elemental magic. It was the fastest way to cause maximum damage. I lowered my eyes away from the fighting, focusing solely on the task before me.

As I unleashed my power, causing the earth to shake, windows to shatter, and large gashes to open up in the street, I attempted to keep the bulk of the damage away from where we fought. My main goal was to keep more vampiric soldiers from flooding the area. We could figure out a way to kill them all after we had a safe space to regroup.

I hadn't anticipated that the mountain the city had been built on was made of stone that was harder than diamonds. Sweat dripped off my brow as I pushed more power into my assault. I needed to cut deeper, wider.

"Godsdammit, kitten!" Thorne bellowed by my side.

My attention snapped and the ground became silent and still once more. I blinked up at the shifter, my limbs suddenly feeling numb. My lungs worked overtime in an effort to supply my body with much needed oxygen.

"Winta! Watch after the idiot king! I need to take care of Ashera!" Thorne called over his shoulder.

I blinked and looked around. We had a small space to ourselves, the fighting had moved closer to the edges I'd gouged into the earth. My bones liquified, and I started to slump to the ground.

"Fucking hell, woman," Thorne snarled. "You need to feed. Can you bulk drain again?"

I shook my head. I didn't have enough energy for that. Hell, I was fighting to keep my eyes open. Each time my eyes closed, it took longer and longer for them to open again. I'd need to rest before I could feed that way again.

"I swear, I'm going to redden your ass, kitten." Thorne gently situated me on the ground and started to remove my clothes. "I'm going to touch you and myself. You're going to feed off that energy. You hear me?"

I nodded. Ambrose be damned.

"I'll allow it if you save her ass!" Ambrose yelled over the fighting. I needed to remember to smack his bitch ass when I was up and moving again.

Thorne ripped his clothes off before he leaned down and pressed a soft kiss against my lips. "Just hang in there, kitten. I'm going to take care of you."

His lips trailed down my throat as my heart beat wildly in my chest. I hated that Thorne was finally getting to touch me, and it was under such horrible circumstances. Yet another reason to rip Tomas's head from his miserable body. The lap of a rough tongue against my nipple tore my thoughts from Tomas and drew them squarely back to Thorne, where they should have been from the start.

A gasp tore from my lips as his fingers trailed down my stomach before sliding between my legs. Thorne circled my clit with the tip of a finger, causing my hips to arch in a silent plea. I felt his arousal spike seconds later and realized by the motion of his shoulders that he was stroking himself.

I moaned, desperately wishing that my arms would move so I could touch him myself.

"Shh, kitten, it's okay. Let me touch you," Thorne's lips moving against my nipple as he spoke sent bolts of pleasure right to my core.

"Please," I mumbled.

"You don't need to beg this time, kitten."

He positioned himself over me, allowing his cock to bump against my clit. I gasped and arched my hips more, needing to feel his hot flesh slide against my own. He chuckled and eased his hips back, moving the hand that had been teasing me to my hips, where he pressed them down to keep me at bay.

Would the army think less of me if I started crying?

Thorne pressed a light kiss against my neck, a purr starting in his chest. "Feed, kitten."

Oh...right.

I started to pull on the sexual energy Thorne was creating, my body slowly coming back to life with each pull I took. My shifter went back to teasing every inch of my body he could get his hands and mouth on as I continued to sip from him as though he were a fine wine. I opened up my empathic gifts just enough to read him, and what I felt floored me.

Devotion. Adoration. Relief. He was so focused on making sure that I was okay, on doing right by me as his mate, that he honestly wasn't thinking about himself at all during this moment between us. My heart swelled.

When I finally found enough energy to move my limbs, I latched onto Thorne's broad frame. My nails dug into his muscular shoulders, and my legs wrapped around his waist. Our gazes locked as I smirked up at him.

"I'm never letting you go, *kitten*," I whispered before burying my hands in his hair and pulling his head down for a kiss.

He growled low against my lips, quickly taking over the kiss and thrusting his tongue into my mouth. They dueled as my hands began to roam over his back, my nails digging into the flesh causing him to hiss against my lips in pleasure.

One of his hands came up and wrapped around my throat, breaking the kiss and he pressed me back against the ground. His eyes blazed with heat as he studied me.

"You're going to fuck me, Thorne. And you're going to do it right the fuck now." I grinned up at him.

His eyes narrowed as he lowered his head to brush his lips against my collarbone. "I'll fuck you, kitten. I know you need my cock buried in your sweet, tight pussy. But make no mistake. I will claim you properly the second we're safe. I'm going to fuck you for *days*. Until all you can think about is how good my cock feels, how wet you get for me, and how crazed you go when I make you come."

I licked my lip and ground my hips against his. I needed to feel him inside me. Gods, I needed it more than I needed my next breath.

The fingers of his other hand found my clit again, stroking it until my legs relaxed and slid from his hips. He chuckled against my chest before sliding a finger into my pussy.

"So fucking wet, kitten. What a good girl." I clamped down around his fingers. "Does someone like knowing she's a good little kitten, getting wet for her mate?"

I apparently really appreciated the praise because I could feel myself getting wetter as I clenched tighter around Thorne's fingers. He groaned.

"Yes, kitten. Squeeze my fingers just like that." He started to thrust them slowly into me, his thumb finding my clit and pressing light circles around it. "I wish I could tease you more, show you just want a good girl you can really be for me. But we don't have time right now."

I whimpered when he pulled his fingers from my aching pussy. He just shot me a cocky smirk before the tip of his dick rubbed against my opening.

"Now take my cock. Every. Inch." Thorne eased in, and I moaned.

Gods, he was huge! Much larger than my other mates. And...I cried out as the first ridge of his cock pushed back my opening. Holy shit. He was ribbed? I'd heard rumors that some shifters had textured cocks, but I hadn't believed them.

I should have fucking believed them.

Thorne paused and looked down at me, studying my reaction. Seeing me half crazed out of my mind for him, he smirked before sliding the rest of the way into me. My eyes rolled into the back of my head. Even filled with multiple mates, I'd never been stretched like this before.

He pulled out slightly before sliding back in.

Holy. Fuck. There was a ridge at the base of his cock that bumped just right against my clit. I clenched down against his dick and released a strangled moan. He was going to kill me.

I blinked my eyes open when Thorne leaned back, his hand still wrapped around my neck, to watch as he slowly slid almost entirely out of me before pushing back all the way.

"Such. A. Good. Fucking. Girl." Thorne snarled, each word punctuated by a thrust of his hips. "Taking all of me. So fucking tight. So fucking wet.

I came. Perhaps I should have been embarrassed that his praise was what really sent me over the edge, but I didn't care. I came, crying out his name.

"Yes," he hissed. "Come on my cock just like that again, kitten. Come again for me and I'll fill you up."

I nodded my head, unable to form words. He leaned down to lick my ear. "Good. Girl."

He slammed into me, his pace turning furiously fast. All I could think about was the bump of one ridge against my g-spot and the bump of the other against my clit. I could hear my voice chanting something, but I wasn't aware of what I was saying. I kept replaying Thorne's praise on repeat as he pounded away inside me.

"I need you to come for me, kitten. Now. Squeeze my cock so hard I won't be able to pull out of you."

I detonated. Stars flooded my vision as I screamed. I heard Thorne's roar as he came moments after me, his hips jerking with his release.

My chest heaved as I came down from my high, my gaze focusing on the large shifter still looming over me. He'd propped himself on his arms so as not to crush me under his weight, though truth be told I would have loved it.

We stared at one another for a long moment before the burning pain started. Mine was right at the center of my chest between my breasts. I glanced down, three slash marks appearing. How apt.

Thorne sat back, glancing down at his thigh. Almost as large as Ambrose's mark, Thorne's mate mark wrapped nearly around his entire left thigh. I wanted to lick it.

"If you're done!" Ambrose yelled. "We need some help here!"

Thankfully, I'd been feeding the entire time we'd been fucking each other. I felt more normal than I had. I'd at least be able to hold my own for a bit.

"Fanged fucker is going to lose his fucking fangs," Thorne snarled before standing and offering me his hand. I laughed as he pulled me up. He handed me my clothes before putting his on. "Are you okay, kitten?"

"I am...thanks to you." My shifter shot me a heated look as he continued to dress. He paused, his eyes darkening as he tangled a hand in my hair, pulling me flush against him.

"I'm going to have him eating my come out of you next time, kitten."

"I look forward to it."

Thorne turned away to grab his weapons.

That was all the time needed. Searing pain ripped through my back. I cried out as the blade that had struck me was yanked free. I spun, coming face to face with Judah.

I knew this fucker was going to be a problem.

A murderous gleam shone bright in his eyes as he wrapped a hand around my neck. "Long live the queen," he whispered.

I blinked, and where Judah had been standing, now stood Daimon. His back was to me and his wings were flared. I could feel the rage radiating off his body, no need for my angelic gifts.

"Long live Queen Ashera," Daimon said.

Daimon

THE IMPOSTER FELL dead at my feet, my hand holding his still beating heart. I'd come this far and wasn't about to fail now. Not when I was so damn close. Not when *we* were so damn close.

I looked up from the heart in my hands to see the others around me all staring at me in shock. I shot Ashera a flirtatious smirk.

"That's not the real Judah anyway," I explained.

"I'm sorry," she replied, blinking at me. "What?"

I kicked the corpse of Judah's twin brother. "This isn't Judah. It's his brother."

"That fuck-nugget!" Winta yelled. "I knew there was something off about him!"

"Yes, well...It wasn't him at all," I said cheerfully. I was still getting weird looks from everyone around me. "You know, I did just save your life."

"Thank you," Ashera said slowly. Her gaze was bouncing between me and the dead body at my feet. "You're sure that isn't Judah?"

"Quite." I nodded. "Now your other two mates are about to inundate the city with Juniyan forces. It should be quite a show."

"What the *fuck* are you?" Ambrose asked.

"I'm a god." I smirked. "And so is our lovely Ashera."

ABOUT THE AUTHOR

Beth is a loving wife and mother—both of the human and fur variety—best friend, enemy, *that* coworker, work wife, hero, all around sarcastic badass, and self-proclaimed Queen of Smut. She advocates to get rid of the stigma around mental health—having CPTSD, anxiety, depression, and panic. She advocates for the understanding of ADHD in girls and women, having ADHD herself, and she wasn't diagnosed until she was thirty. When she isn't writing, she's playing with her young son, getting sassy with her husband, reading with the cats, roughhousing with the doggo, or sleeping for days. She loves to hear from fans and makes an effort to answer any messages sent her way and like any posts she's tagged in.

Make sure to follow me on:
- Instagram: @authorelizabethbrown
- Twitter: @authorelizabet3
- TikTok: RomanceAuthorBethBrown
- Facebook Group: Beth's Resurrected Queens
- Subscribe to my website: authorelizabethbrown.com
- Feel free to shoot me an email: authorelizabethbrown@gmail.com

ALSO BY ELIZABETH BROWN

The Resurrection of Queens Series

Discovery of a Queen (The Resurrection of Queens, Book 1) — Now available on all platforms!

Vengeance of a Queen (The Resurrection of Queens, Book 2) — Now available on all platforms

Power of a Queen (The Resurrection of Queens, Book 3)—Coming April 20, 2022

∽

Freedom's Harem Trilogy

Blood Crown—Now available on all platforms!

War Crown—Now available on all platforms!

Immortal Crown—Coming 2022

∽

Standalones

Weaving Fate—Coming December 23, 2021